THE WINDS OF LIMBO

Michael Moorcock is astonishing. His enormous output includes around fifty novels, innumerable short stories and a rock album. Born in London in 1939, he became editor of *Tarzan Adventures* at sixteen, moving on later to edit the *Sexton Blake Library*. He has earned his living as a writer/editor ever since, and is without doubt one of Britain's most popular and most prolific authors. He has been compared with Tennyson, Tolkien, Raymond Chandler, Wyndham Lewis, Ronald Firbank, Mervyn Peake, Edgar Allan Poe, Colin Wilson, Anatole France, William Burroughs, Edgar Rice Burroughs, Charles Dickens, James Joyce, Vladimir Nabokov, Jorge Luis Borges, Joyce Cary, Ray Bradbury, H G Wells, George Bernard Shaw and Hieronymus Bosch, among others.

'No one at the moment in England is doing more to break down the artificial divisions that have grown up in novel writing – realism, surrealism, science fiction, historical fiction, social satire, the poetic novel – than Michael Moorcock'
Angus Wilson

'He is an ingenious and energetic experimenter, restlessly original, brimming over with clever ideas'
Robert Nye, *The Guardian*

Also by Michael Moorcock

The Cornelius Chronicles
The Final Programme
A Cure for Cancer
The English Assassin
The Condition of Muzak
*The Lives and Times of Jerry
    Cornelius*
*The Adventures of Una Persson
    and Catherine Cornelius in
    the Twentieth Century*

The Dancers at the End of Time
An Alien Heat
The Hollow Lands
The End of All Songs
Legends from the End of Time
*The Transformation of Miss
    Mavis Ming (Return of the
    Fireclown)*

Hawkmoon: The History of
    the Runestaff
The Jewel in the Skull
The Mad God's Amulet
The Sword of the Dawn
The Runestaff

Hawkmoon: The Chronicles
    of Castle Brass
Count Brass
The Champion of Garathorm*
The Quest for Tanelorn*

Erekosë
The Eternal Champion
Phoenix in Obsidian
The Champion of Garathorm*
The Quest for Tanelorn*

Elric Series
Elric of Melniboné
The Sailor on the Seas of Fate
The Sleeping Sorceress

* Interconnected series

The Stealer of Souls
Stormbringer
Elric at the End of Time

The Books of Corum
The Knight of the Swords
The Queen of the Swords
The King of the Swords
The Bull and the Spear
The Oak and the Ram
The Sword and the Stallion

Other Titles
The City of the Beast
The Lord of the Spiders
The Masters of the Pit
The Warlord of the Air
The Land Leviathan
Behold the Man
Breakfast in the Ruins
The Blood-Red Game
The Black Corridor
The Chinese Agent
The Distant Suns
The Rituals of Infinity
The Shores of Death
Sojan the Swordsman (juvenile)
The Golden Barge
*Gloriana (or, the Unfulfill'd
    Queene, a Romance)*
The Time Dweller (short
    stories)
Moorcock's Book of Martyrs
    (short stories)
Entropy Tango
Heroic Dreams (non-fiction)

Michael Moorcock

The Winds of Limbo

A MAYFLOWER BOOK

GRANADA
London Toronto Sydney New York

Published by Granada Publishing Limited in 1974
Reprinted 1976, 1980

ISBN 0 583 12338 4

First published in Great Britain as THE FIRECLOWN
by Compact Books 1965
Copyright © Michael Moorcock 1965

Granada Publishing Limited
Frogmore, St Albans, Herts AL2 2NF
and
3 Upper James Street, London W1R 4BP
866 United Nations Plaza, New York, NY 10017, USA
117 York Street, Sydney, NSW 2000, Australia
100 Skyway Avenue, Rexdale, Ontario, M9W 3A6, Canada
PO Box 84165, Greenside, 2034 Johannesburg, South Africa
61 Beach Road, Auckland, New Zealand

Printed and bound in Great Britain by
Hazell Watson & Viney Ltd,
Aylesbury, Bucks
Set in Linotype Times

CHAPTER ONE

IT WAS a vast cavern. Part of it was natural, part of it had been hollowed out by the machines of men. Some parts were deep in dancing shadow and others were brilliantly illuminated by a great blazing mass—a roaring, crackling miniature replica of the sun itself, that hung, constantly quivering and erupting, near the high roof.

Beneath this blazing orb a tall column rose up as if to meet it, and arms akimbo upon a platform at the top stood a gross figure, clad in ragged, harlequin costume. A soft, floppy, conical hat was jammed over his lank, yellow hair; his fat-rounded face was painted white, his eyes and mouth adorned with smears of red, yellow and black, and on the ragged red jerkin stretched taut upon his great belly was a vivid yellow sunburst.

Below this gross harlequin the dense crowd surrounding the column ceased its movement as he raised an orange hand that seemed to shoot from his torn sleeve like fingers of flame.

He laughed. It was as if the sun had voiced unearthly humour.

"Speak to us!" the crowd pleaded. "Fireclown! Speak to us!"

He ceased his laughing and looked down at them with a peculiar expression moving behind the paint. At length he bellowed:

"I am the Fireclown!"

"Speak to us!"

"I am the Fireclown, equipped for your salvation. I am the gift bearer, alive with the Fire of Life, from which the Earth itself was formed! I am the Earth's brother. . . ."

A woman in a padded dress representing the body of a lion cried shrilly: "And what are we?"

"You are maggots feeding off your mother. When you mate it is like corpses coupling. When you laugh it is the sound of the winds of limbo!"

"Why? Why?" shouted a young man with a lean, mean face and a pointed chin that could pierce a throat. He leapt exuberantly while his eyes glinted and looked.

"You have shunned the natural life and worshipped the artificial. But you are not lost—not yet!"

7

"What shall we do?" sobbed a government official, sweating in the purple jacket and purple pantaloons of his rank, caught by the ritual enough to fidget and forget to stay in the shadows. His cry was echoed by the crowd.

"What shall we do?"

"Follow me! I will reinstate you as Children of the Sun and Brothers of the Earth. Spurn me—and you perish in your artificiality, renounced by Nature on whom you have turned your proud backs."

And again the clown broke into a laugh. He breathed heavily and roared his insane and enigmatic humour at the cavern roof. Flames from the suspended miniature sun leapt, stretched and shot out, as if to kiss the Fireclown's acolytes who laughed and shouted, surging about him, applauding him.

The Fireclown looked down as he laughed, drinking in their adoration.

In a shadow cast by the dais, detached from the milling crowd, a gaunt Negro stood as if petrified, his eyelids painted in checks of red and white, his mouth coloured green. He wore an extravagant yellow cut-away coat and scarlet tights. He looked up at the Fireclown and there were tears of hunger in his eyes. The Negro's name was Junnar.

The faces of the crowd were lashed and slashed by the leaping fire, some eyes dull, some bright, some eyes blind and some hot, overloaded with heat.

Many of the figures wore masks moulded in plastic to caricature their own faces—long noses, no noses, slit eyes, cow eyes, lipless mouths, gaping mouths. Some were painted in gaudy colours, others were naked and some wore padded clothes representing animals or plants.

Here they gathered around the dais. Many hundreds of them, loving the man who capered like a jester above them, lashing them with his wriggling rhetoric, laughing, laughing. Scientists, pick-pockets, spacemen, explorers, musicians, confidence tricksters, blackmailers, poets, doctors, whores, murderers, clerks, perverts, government officials, spies, policemen, social workers, beggars, actors, politicians, riff-raff.

Here they all were. And they shouted. And as they shouted the gross Fool capered yet more wildly and the flame responded frenetically to his dancing and his own wordless cries.

"The Fireclown!" they sobbed.

"The Fireclown!" they bellowed.

8

"The Fireclown! The Fireclown!" they howled and laughed.

"The Fireclown!" He giggled and he danced like a madman's puppet upon his dais and sang his mirth.

All this, in the lowest level of the multi-storied labyrinth that was the City of Switzerland.

With a great effort the Negro Junnar turned his eyes away from the Fireclown, stumbled backwards, wrenched his body round and ran for one of the black exits, bent on leaving before he was completely trapped by the Fireclown's spell.

Behind him, the sound of the maddened crowd diminished as he ran along fusty, ill-smelling corridors until he could no longer hear it. Then he began to walk up ramps and stairs until he came to an escalator. He stepped on to the escalator and let himself be taken up to the top, a hundred feet from the bottom. This corridor was also deserted, but better lighted and cleaner that those he had left. He looked up and found a sign at an intersection:

> NINTH LEVEL (Mechanics) Hogarth Lane—Leading to Divebomber Street and Orangeblossom Road (Elevators to Forty Levels)

He made for Orangeblossom Road, an old residential corridor but very sparsely inhabited these days, found the elevators at the end, pressed a button and waited impatiently for five minutes before one arrived. He entered it and rose non-stop to the forty-ninth level. Outside he crossed the bright, bustling corridor and got into a crowded lift bound for the sixty-fifth— the topmost—level.

The liveried operator recognized him and said deferentially: "Any tips for when the next election's going to be held, Mr. Junnar?"

Junnar, abstracted, tried to smile politely. He shook his head. "Tomorrow, if the RLMs had their way," he said. "But we're not worried. People have faith in the Solrefs." He frowned. He had caught himself using a party slogan again. Apparently the operator hadn't noticed, but Junnar thought he saw a hint of irony in the man's eyes. He ignored it, frowned again, this time for a different reason. Obviously people were *losing* faith in the Solar Referendum Party. A sign of the times, he thought.

At length the elevator reached the sixty-fifth level and the operator called out conscientiously: "Sixty-five. Please show appointment cards as you go through the barrier."

The people began to shuffle out, some towards transport that would take them right across the vast plateau of the Top Level, some towards the distant buildings comprising the Seat of Government, various Ministries and the private accommodations of important statesmen, politicians and civil servants.

Built with the money of frightened businessmen during the war scares of the 1970s, the city had grown upwards and outwards so that it now covered almost two-thirds of what was once the country of Switzerland—one vast building. A warren with mountains embedded in it, it had begun as a warren of super-shelters *below* the mountains. The war scares had died down, but the city had remained along with the businessmen and, when the World Government was formed in 2005, it seemed the natural place for the capital. In 2031, in a bid to get full rights of citizenship for outworld settlers, the Solar Referendum Party had been formed. Four years later it had risen to power. Its first act had been to declare that from henceforth they were a Solar Government running the affairs of the Federation of Solar Planets.

But since then more than sixty years had passed. The Solrefs had lost much of their original dynamism, having become the most powerfully conservative party in the Solar House.

The official at the barrier knew Junnar and waved him through. Sun poured in through the glass-alloy dome far above his head and the artificially scented air was refreshing after the untainted stuff of the middle levels and the impure air of the lowest.

He walked across the turf-covered plaza, listening to the splashing fountains that at intervals glinted among beds of exotic flowers. He was struck by the contrast between the hot excitement, the smell of sweat and the surge of bodies he had just left, and this cool, well-controlled expanse, artificially maintained yet as beautiful as anything nature could produce.

But he did not pause to savour the view. His pace was hurried compared with the movement of the few other people who sauntered with dignity along the paths. At a distance, the tall white, blue and silver buildings of the ambiguously named Private Level reflected the sun and enhanced the atmosphere of calm and assurance of the Top.

Junnar crossed the plaza and walked up a clean, gravelled

path towards the wide stone arch that opened on to a shady court. Around this court many windows looked down upon the cool pool in its centre. Goldfish glinted in the pool. At the archway, a porter left his lodge and planted himself on the path until Junnar reached him. He was a sour-faced man, dressed in a dark grey blouse and pantaloons; he looked at Junnar with vague disapproval as the flamboyant Negro stopped and produced his pass, sighing: "Here you are, Drew. You're very conscientious today."

"My job is to check all passes, sir."

Junnar smiled at him. "You don't recognize me, is that it."

"I recognize you very well, sir, but it would be more than my job's worth to ..."

"Let me in without checking my pass," Junnar finished for him. "You're an annoying man, Drew."

The porter didn't reply. He was not afraid of incurring Junnar's disapproval since he had a strong union that would be only too ready to take up cudgels on his behalf if he was fired without adequate grounds.

So temporarily disorientated was Junnar that he allowed this tiny conflict to carry him further, and as he went into the court he shrugged and said: "It's better to have friends than enemies, though, Drew ..." Immediately he felt foolish.

He took out a pack of proprietary brand marijuanas and lit one as he went through a glass-panelled door into the quiet, deserted hall of the building. The hall was lined with mirrors. He stood staring at himself in one of them, drawing deeply on the sweet smoke, collecting his thoughts and pulling himself together. This was the third time he had attended one of the Fireclown's 'audiences' and each time the Clown's magnetism had drawn him closer and the atmosphere of the great cavern had affected him more profoundly. He didn't want his employer to notice that.

After a moment's contemplation Junnar went to the central glass panel which was on the right and withdrew a small oblong box from his pocket. He put it close to his mouth.

"Junnar," he said.

The panel slid back to reveal a black, empty shaft. There was a peculiar dancing quality about the blackness. Junnar stepped into it and, instantaneously, was opening the inner door of a cabinet. He walked out and the door closed behind him. He was in a corridor lighted by windows that stretched

11

from floor to ceiling and showed in the distance the thick banks of summer cloud far below.

Immediately opposite him was a great door of red-tinted chrome. It now opened silently.

In the big, beautiful room, two men awaited him. One was young, one was old; both showed physical similarities, both appeared impatient.

Junnar entered the room and dropped his cigarette into a disposal column.

"Good afternoon, sir," he said to the old man, and nodded to the young man. "Good afternoon, Mr. Powys."

The old man spoke, his voice rich and resonant. "Well, Junnar, what's happening down there now?"

CHAPTER TWO

ALAN POWYS fingered the case of papers under his arm, studying his grandfather and the painted Negro as they confronted one another. They made a strange pair.

Minister Simon Powys was tall and heavy without much obvious fat, but his face was as grim and disturbing as an Easter Island god's. The leonine set of his head was further enhanced by the flowing mane of white hair which reached almost to his shoulders, hanging straight as if carved. He wore the standard purple suit of a high-ranking cabinet minister—he was Minister for Space Transport, an important office—pleated jacket, padded pantaloons, red stockings and white pumps. His white shirt was open at the neck to reveal old but firm flesh, and on his breast was a golden star, symbol of his rank.

Junnar was sighing and spreading his hands. "If you, Minister Powys, want to stop him you should act now. His power increases daily. People are flocking to him. He *seems* harmless, insofar as he doesn't appear to have any great political ambitions, but his power could be used to threaten society's stability."

"Could be? I'm sure it *will* be." Minister Powys spoke heavily. "But can we convince parliament of the danger? There's the irony."

"Probably not." Alan Powys spoke distantly, conscious of an

12

outsider's presence. He thought he glimpsed, momentarily, a strange expression on the Negro's face.

"Helen and that mob of rabble-rousers she calls a political party are only too pleased to encourage him," Minister Powys grumbled. "Not to mention certain members of the government who seem as fascinated by him as schoolgirls on their first dates." He straightened his shoulders which were beginning to stoop with old age. "There must be some way of showing them their mistake."

Alan Powys chose not to argue with his grandfather in Junnar's presence. Personally, however, he thought the old man over-emphasized the Fireclown's importance. Perhaps Junnar sensed this, for he said softly:

"The Fireclown has a certain ability to attract and hold interest. The most unlikely people seem to have come under his spell. His magnetism is intense and almost irresistible. Have you been to one of his 'audiences' Mr. Powys?"

Alan shook his head.

"Then go to one—before you judge. Believe me, he has *something*. He's more than a crank."

Alan wondered why the normally self-possessed and taciturn Negro should choose to speak in this way. Perhaps one day he would attend a meeting. He certainly was curious.

"Who is he, anyway?" Alan asked as his grandfather paced towards the window comprising the outer wall of the room.

"No one knows," Junnar said. "His origins, like his theories, are obscure. He will not tell anyone his real name. There are no records of his fingerprints at Identity Centre; he seems demented, but no mental hospital has heard of him. Perhaps, as he says, he came down from the sun to save the world?"

"Don't be facetious, Junnar." Minister Powys pursed his lips, paused, then took a long breath and said: "Who was down there today?"

"Vernitz, Chief of the China Police—he is in the city on a vacation and to attend the Police Conference next Sixday. Martha Gheld, Professor of Electrobiology at Tel Aviv. All the Persian representatives currently elected to parliament . . ."

"Including Isfahan?" Minister Powys was too well bred to shout, but there was astonishment in his voice. Isfahan was the leader of the Solref faction in the Solar House.

"Including all the Persian Solrefs, I'm afraid." Junnar

13

nodded. "Not to mention a number of Dutch, Swedish and Mexican party members."

"We had advised our members not to take part in the Fireclown's farcical 'audiences'!"

"Doubtless they were all there on fact-finding missions," Alan interrupted, a faint gleam in his eyes.

"Doubtless," Powys said grimly, choosing to ignore his grandson's irony.

"Your niece was there, too," Junnar said quietly.

"That doesn't surprise me. The woman's a fool. To think that she could be the next President!"

Alan knew that his cousin, Helen Curtis, leader of the Radical Liberal Movement, and his grandfather were both planning to run for President in the forthcoming Presidential elections. One of them was sure to win.

"All right, Junnar." Simon Powys dismissed his secretary. The Negro went out through a side door opening on an inner passage leading to his own office.

When the door had closed, Alan said: "I think you place too much importance on this character, grandfather. He's harmless enough. Perhaps he could threaten society—but it's doubtful if he would. You seem to have an obsession about him. No one else, in politics at least, seems so concerned. If the situation became serious people would soon leave him or act against him. Why not wait and see?"

"No. I seem to have an obsession, do I? Well, it may be that I'm the only man not blinded to what this Fireclown represents. I have already drafted a Bill which, if it gets passed, could easily put a stop to the fool's posturing."

Alan laid his briefcase on the desk and sat down in one of the deep armchairs. "But will it? Surely it isn't wise at this stage to back what could easily be an unpopular motion. The Fireclown is an attractive figure to most people—and as yet harmless. If you were to oppose him openly it might cost you votes in the Presidential election. You could lose it!"

Alan felt he had scored a point. He knew how important winning was to the old man. Since the formation of the Solar Referendum Party, a Powys of every generation had held the Presidential chair for at least one term of his life—a Powys had in fact formed the first Solref cabinet. Yet it was likely the Powys would not be voted in, for public opinion was gradually going against the Solrefs and tending to favour the more vociferous and dynamic RLM, which had grown rapidly in strength under Helen Curtis's fiery leadership. Throughout his life Simon Powys had aimed at the Presidency, and this would be his last chance to gain it.

"I have never sacrificed principles for mere vote-catching!" Simon Powys said scornfully. "It is unworthy of a Powys to suggest it, Alan. Your mother would have been horrified if she had heard such a remark coming from her own son. Though you have the look of a Powys, the blood, whoever gave it you, is not Powys blood!"

For a second before he controlled himself, Alan felt pain at this remark. This was the first time his grandfather had referred to his obscure origins—he had been illegitimate, his mother dying soon after he was born. Though, in his grim way, Simon Powys had assured his grandson's education and position, he had always been withdrawn from Alan, caring for him but not encouraging friendship or love. His wife had died five years earlier and she and Alan had been close. When Eleanor Powys died Simon had begun to see a little more of Alan, but had always remained slightly distant. However, this remark about his bastardy was the first spoken in anger. Obviously the matter of the Presidency was weighing on his mind.

Alan ignored the elder Powys' reference and smiled.

"City Administration—if I may return to the original topic —isn't worried by the Fireclown. He inhabits the disused lower levels and gives us no trouble, doesn't threaten to come upstairs at all. Leave him alone, grandfather—at least until after the election."

Minister Simon went to the picture window and stared out into the twilight, his erect body silhouetted against the distant mountains.

"The Fireclown is a tangible threat, Alan. He has admitted that he is bent on the destruction of our whole society, on the rejection of all its principles of progress and democracy. With his babbling of fire-worship and nature-worship, the Fireclown threatens to throw us all back to disorganized and retrogressive savagery!"

"Grandfather—the man isn't that powerful! You place too much importance on him!"

Simon Powys shook his head, his heavy hands clasping behind him.

"I say I do not!"

15

"Then you are wrong!" Alan said angrily, half aware that his anger was not so much inspired by the old man's righteousness as by his earlier, wounding remark.

Simon Powys remained with his back to Alan, silent.

At least his grandfather's solid reputation for integrity and sticking to what he thought was well earned, Alan reflected. But that reputation might not save him if the Fireclown became a political issue in the elections.

His own view, shared with a great many people, was that the Fireclown's mysterious appearance a year ago was welcome as an agent to relieve the comparative monotony of running the smoothly ordered City of Switzerland.

"Goodbye, grandfather," he said, picking up his briefcase. "I'm going home. I've got a lot of work to get through this evening."

Simon Powys turned—a considered and majestic movement.

"You may like to know that I have approached the City Council on this matter, suggesting that they completely seal off the lower levels. I hope they will adopt my suggestion. City Administration, of course, would be responsible for carrying it out. As Assistant Director, you would probably be in charge of the project."

"If the City Council have any sense they'll ignore your suggestion. They have no evidence of law-breaking on the Fireclown's part. They can take no legal steps against him. All he has done, so far as I can see, is to address a public meeting—and that isn't a crime in this democracy you've been boasting of. To make it one would invalidate your whole argument. Don't you agree?"

"One short step back could save us from a long slide down," Minister Powys said curtly as Alan left the room.

Entering the elevator that would take him home to the sixty-fourth level, Alan decided that he could have misjudged his grandfather over the matter of the Fireclown. He had heard a great deal about him and his 'audiences' and, emotionally, was attracted by the romantic character of the man. But he had argued the Fireclown's case too strongly without really knowing it at first hand.

He left the elevator and crossed to the middle of the corridor, taking the fastway belt towards his flat. As he neared it, he crossed to the slowway with instinctive practice, produced a

16

small box from his pocket and spoke his name into it. The door of the flat opened in the wall.

In the passage his manservant took his briefcase and carried it into the study. "We were expecting you home earlier, sir. Madeleine apologizes, but she feels the polter may be over-done."

"My fault, Stefanos." He was not particularly fond of synthetic poultry, anyway.

"And Miss Curtis is waiting for you in the living room. I told her you hadn't dined . . ."

"That's all right." Outwardly decisive, he was inwardly confused. He even felt a slight trembling in his legs and cursed himself for an uncontrolled buffoon. He had only once seen Helen, briefly, since their affair had ended, at a party.

He entered the austere living room.

"Good evening, Helen. How are you?"

They did not shake hands.

"Hello, Alan."

He could not guess why she was here but he did not particularly want to know. He was afraid he might get involved emotionally with her again.

He sat down. She seated herself opposite him in the other padded, armless chair. She was made up—which was unusual. Her lips were a light green and she had on some sort of ultra-white powder. Her eyebrows and eyelids were red. Her taste, he thought, had never been all it might. She had an almost triangular face; short, black hair and a small nose so that she looked rather like a cat—save for the make-up which made her look like a corpse.

"I hear you attended the Fireclown's 'audience' today?" he said casually.

"Where did you hear that? Bush telegraph? Have you been at a cocktail party?"

"No." He smiled half-heartedly. "But spies are everywhere these days."

"You've been to see uncle Simon, then? Is he planning to use the information against me in the election?"

"I don't think so—no."

She was evidently nervous. Her voice was shaking slightly. Probably his own was, too. They had been very close—in love, even—and the break, when it had finally come, had been made in anger. He had not been alone with her since.

17

"What do you think your chances are of winning it?"

She smiled. "Good."

"Yes, they seem to be."

"Will you be pleased?"

She knew very well that he wouldn't be. Her political ambitions had been the main reasons for their parting. Unlike all the rest of his family, including remote cousins, he had no interest in politics. Maybe, he thought with a return of his earlier bitterness, Simon Powys had been right about his blood being inherited from his unknown father. He shook his head, shrugging slightly, smiling vaguely.

"I—I don't know," he lied. Of course he would be disappointed if she won. He hated the political side of her character. Where as he had nothing against women in politics—it would have been atavistic and unrealistic if he had an objection—he felt that her talents lay elsewhere. Perhaps in the painting she no longer had time for? She had been, potentially, a very fine painter.

"It's time the Solar System had a shake-up," she said. "The Solrefs have been in for too long."

"Probably," he said non-committally. Then, desperate to get it over: "Why are you here, Helen?"

"I wanted some help."

"What kind of help? Personal . . . ?"

"No, of course not. Don't worry. When you said it was over I believed you. I've still got the mark on my shoulder."

This had been on his conscience and her reference to it hurt him. He had struck her on her shoulder, not really intending the blow to be hard, but it had been.

"I'm sorry about that . . . ," he said stumblingly. "I didn't mean . . ."

"I know. I shouldn't have brought it up." She smiled and said quickly: "Actually, I want some information, Alan. I know that you're politically uncommitted, so I'm sure you won't mind giving it to me."

"But I don't have any *secrets,* Helen. I'm not in that position —I'm only a civil servant, you know that."

"It's not really a secret. All I want is some—what d'you call it?—advance information."

"About what?"

"I heard a rumour that the City Council plan to close off the lower levels. Is that true?"

"I really couldn't say, Helen." News was travelling fast. Obviously an indiscreet councillor had mentioned Simon Powys's letter to someone and this had been the start of the rumour. On the other hand, his grandfather, when he told him of it, had understood that he would keep the old man's confidence. He could say nothing—though the truth would put paid to the rumour.

"But you're in City Administration. You must know. You'd be responsible for the project, wouldn't you?"

"If such a project were to be carried out, yes. But I have been told nothing either by the City Council or my Director. I should ignore the rumour. Anyway, why should it bother you?"

"Because if it's true it would be interesting to know which councillors backed the motion, and who egged them on. The only man with sufficient power and a great enough obsession is your grandfather—my uncle, Simon Powys!"

"How many Solar Referendum councillors are in the Council?" he asked vaguely. He was smelling her perfume now. He remembered it with a sad nostalgia. This was becoming too much to bear.

"There are five Solrefs, three RLMs, one independent Socialist and one Crespignite who slipped in somewhere on the pensioner's vote. Giving, if you are so ignorant of simple politics, a majority to the Solrefs and virtual control of the Council, since the Crespignite is bound to vote with them on nearly every issue."

"So you want to tell the people that this hypothetical closing down of the lower levels is a Solref plot—a blow to their liberty."

"My very words," she said with a kind of triumphant complacency.

He got up. "And you expect me to help you—to betray confidence, not to mention giving my own grandfather's opponents extra ammunition—and let you know what the City Council decides before it is made public? You're becoming foolish, Helen. Politics must be addling your brains!"

"But it means nothing to you, anyway. You're not interested in politics!"

"That's so. One of the reasons I'm not interested is because of the crookedness that seems to get into the best of people—people who think any means to win elections are fair! I'm not naïve, Helen. I'm from the same family as you. I grew up knowing politics. That's why I stay out of it!"

"Surely you don't support this victimization of the Fireclown, Alan? He is a simple, spontaneous . . ."

"I'm not interested in hearing a list of the Fireclown's virtues. And whether I support any 'victimization', as you call it, is of no importance. As a matter of fact, I'm attracted to the Fireclown and consider him no danger at all. But it seems to me that both you and grandfather are using this man for your own political ends, and I'll have no part of it!" He paused, considering what he had said, then added: "Finally, there has been no 'victimization', and there isn't likely to be!"

"That's what you think. I support the Fireclown for good reasons. His ambitions and the ambitions of the RLM are linked. He wants to bring sanity and real life back to this machine-ridden world. We want real values back again!"

"Oh, God!" He shook his head impatiently. "Helen, I've got a great deal of work to do before I go to bed tonight."

"Very well. I have, too. If you reconsider . . ."

"Even if there was a plot to *arrest* the Fireclown I wouldn't tell you so that you could use it for political fuel, Helen." He suddenly found himself moving towards her, gripping her arm. "Listen. Why get involved with this? You've got a good chance of winning the election without indulging in dealings of this sort. Wait until you're President, then you can make the Fireclown into a Solar Trust if you like!"

"You can't understand," she said grimly, shaking herself free of his hand. "You don't realize that you have to be comparatively ruthless when you know what you're aiming for is *right*."

"Then I'm glad you know what's right," he said pityingly. "I'm bloody glad you know. It's more than I do."

She left in silence and he went back to his chair, slumping down heavily and feeling, with morose pleasure, that he had scored.

The mood didn't last long. By the time Stefanos came in to tell him his meal was waiting for him he had sunk into a brooding, unconstructive melancholy. Brusquely he told his manservant to eat the meal himself and then go out for the rest of the evening.

"Thank you, sir," Stefanos said wonderingly, chewing his ridged underlip as he left the room.

In this mood in which his confrontation of his ex-mistress had left him, Alan felt incapable of work. The work was of little real importance anyway, routine stuff which he had hoped to clear up before he took his vacation in a fortnight's time. He decided to go to bed, hoping that a good ten hours' sleep would help him forget Helen.

He had reached the point where he felt he must see the mysterious figure for himself, since so many matters seemed to be revolving around him all of a sudden.

He walked into the darkened hall and ordered the light on. The light responded to his voice and flooded the flat. The tiny escalator leading upstairs began to move, too, and he stepped on it, letting it carry him to the landing.

He went into his bedroom. It was as sparsely furnished as the rest of the flat—a bed, mellowlamp for reading, a small shelf of books, a wing on the headboard of the bed for anything he cared to put there, and a concealed wardrobe. The air was fresh from the ventilators, also hidden.

He took off his scarlet jacket and pants, told the wardrobe to open, told the cleaning chute to open and dropped them in. He selected a single-piece sleeping suit and moved moodily to sit on the edge of the bed.

Then he got up and went back to the wardrobe, removed an ordinary suit of street garments and put them on.

Rapidly, feeling that he should have taken something with him—a weapon or a notebook or an alarm signaller which would contact the police wherever he was—he left the flat and took the fastway towards the elevators.

He was going to the lower levels. He was going to find the Fireclown.

CHAPTER THREE

HE WAS unreasoningly annoyed that the liveried operator should recognize him and stare at him curiously as he was taken down to the forty-ninth level. In the back of his mind he was thrilling to the experience, unremembered since boyhood, of exploration. He had chosen nondescript clothes so that he might move about incognito.

He was alone in the unmanned elevator as it dropped swiftly

to the ninth level, causing him the added excitement of being alone and virtually helpless against danger.

He stepped boldly into the ill-lit corridor named—incongruously—Orangeblossom Road, and then advanced cautiously until he saw a sign which read: Escalators (down) five levels.

He rode the escalators into the chilly depths of the City of Switzerland, feeling as if he were descending into some frozen Hell and at the same time making a mental note that if people were, indeed, inhabiting the lower levels, then City Administration should, out of humanity, do something about the heating arrangements.

He wished he had some warmer clothing, but that would have meant applying to Garment Centre, since he rarely went outside save on vacation, and then all necessary apparel was supplied.

But as he advanced deeper he became aware of a growing warmth and a thick, unpleasant smell that he gradually recognized as being, predominantly, the smell of human perspiration. In spite of his revulsion he sniffed it curiously.

As he walked slowly down the ramp leading to the notorious first level, reputed to be the haunt of undesirables well before the Fireclown first made his appearance, he saw with a slight shock that the light was dancing and had an unusual quality about it. As he drew closer his excitement increased. Naked flame! The light came from a great, burning torch which also gave off uncontrolled heat!

He approached it as close as he dared and stared at it, marvelling. He had seen recordings of the phenomenon, but this was the first time . . . He withdrew hastily as the heat produced sweat from his forehead, walking along a corridor that reminded him, with its dancing, naked light, of the fairyland of his childhood fantasies. On reflection, he decided it was more like the ogre's castle, but so delighted was he by this wholly new experience that he forgot caution for a while. It only returned as he rounded another corner and saw that the roof was actually composed of living rock, so moist that it dripped condensed water!

Alan Powys was not an unsophisticated young man, yet this was so remote from his everyday experience that he could not immediately absorb it on any intellectual level.

From ahead came sounds—the sounds of excited human voices. He had expected a vast conclave of some description, but he heard only a few people, and they were conversing. Occasionally, as he drew nearer, he heard a reverberating laugh which seemed to him so full of delighted and profound humour that he wished he knew the joke so that he could join in. If this was the Fireclown's famous laughter, then it did not strike him as at all insane.

Still, he told himself, keeping in the shadows, there were many forms of madness.

A cave came into view on his right. He hugged the left-hand wall and inched forward, his heart pounding.

The cave appeared to turn at a right-angle so that he could only see the light coming from it, but now he could make out fragments of words and phrases. At intervals there came a spluttering eruption of green light and each time he was caught in the flare.

". . . shape it into something we can control . . ."

". . . no good, it's only a hint of what we might . . ."

". . . your eyeshield back. I'm going to . . ."

A hissing eruption and a tongue of green flame seemed to turn the bend in the cave and come flickering like an angry cobra towards Alan. He gasped and stepped back as the roaring laughter followed the eruption. Had he been seen?

No. The conversation was continuing, the pitch of the voices now high with excitement.

He crossed the corridor swiftly and stood in the mouth of the cave, straining his ears to make out what they were talking about.

Then he felt a delicate touch on his arm and heard a whispering voice say: "I'm afraid you can't go in there. Private, you know."

He turned slowly and was horrified at the apparition that still touched his arm. He withdrew, nauseated.

The horrible figure laughed softly. "Serves you right. They could keep me just to stop people nosing around!"

"I didn't know you had any kind of secrecy," Alan babbled. "I really do apologize if . . ."

"We welcome visitors, but we prefer to invite them. You don't mind?" The skinless man nodded towards the corridor. Alan backed into it, forcing himself to ignore the bile in his throat, forcing himself to look at the creature without obvious revulsion—but it was difficult.

Flesh, veins and sinews shone on his body as if the whole

23

outer covering had been peeled off. How could he move? How could he appear so calm?

"My skin's synthetic—but transparent. Something in it takes the place of pigment. They haven't worked out a way of giving the stuff pigmentation yet—I was lucky enough to be the guinea-pig. I could use cosmetics, but I don't. My name's Corso. I'm the Fireclown's trusty henchman and deal with any-one interested in coming to his audiences. You arrived at the wrong time. We had one this afternoon."

Obviously Corso was used to random explorers, particularly those curious about the Fireclown. Deciding to play his part in the role Corso had mistakenly given him, Alan looked down at the floor.

"Oh, I'm sorry. When's the next one?"

"Day after tomorrow."

"I can come then?"

"Very welcome."

Alan turned to retrace his way

"See you then," said the skinless man.

When Alan turned the corner of the corridor he had to lean against the wall for some moments before he could continue. Too many unexpected shocks this evening, he told himself.

As he began to recover his composure his curiosity started to operate again. What was going on? From what he had seen and heard, the Fireclown and a group of his friends were con-ducting some sort of laboratory experiment—and Corso, the skinless man, had been left on guard to turn pryers away.

Well, everyone had a right to their privacy. But his curiosity came close to overwhelming him. He began to return towards the cave when a soft voice that he recognized said:

"It wouldn't be wise. If you went back a second time Corso would know you were no innocent would-be initiate."

"Junnar!" he hissed. "What are you doing here?"

But he heard only a faint scuffling and received no reply.

Perhaps, however, the Negro's advice was good. There was no point in making anyone suspicious since he would, if dis-covered, be excluded from any future chance of seeing the Fireclown.

He began to return toward the ramp. What on earth had Junnar been doing in the lower levels? Was he there on his own business or on Simon Powys's? Perhaps the Negro would tell him tomorrow, if he could find an excuse for leaving the C.A. building and visiting his grandfather's apartment.

Vaguely irritated that he had seen so little of the Fireclown's domain and nothing at all of the Fireclown himself, he finally arrived on the sixty-fourth level, took the fastway to his flat and went to bed with something of his earlier sudden mood eliminated.

The day after tomorrow he would definitely attend the Fireclown's 'audience'.

Very deliberately, the next morning, Alan concentrated his thoughts entirely on his job. By the time he arrived at his office in City Administration on North Top, he had turned his thoughts to the matter of elevator installation which the City Council had decided was necessary to speed up pedestrian flow between levels.

His Assistant Directorship was well earned, but he had to admit that having it was partly due to his family connections and the education which his grandfather had insisted on him having. But he was a hard and conscientious worker who got on well with his staff, and the Director seemed pleased with him. He had been doing the job for two years since he had left the university.

He spent the morning catching up on lost time until just before lunch when Carson, the director, called him into his office.

Carson was a thin man with an unsavoury appearance. He was much respected by those working under him. His chin, however, always looked as if he needed a shave and his swarthy face always appeared to need a wash. But this wasn't his fault. After a little time in his company the first impression of his unsavouriness vanished swiftly.

Carson said mildly: "Sit down, Alan. I wonder if you could leave the elevator matter for a while and turn it over to Sevlin to get on with. Something else has cropped up."

Powys sat down and watched Carson leaf through the papers on his desk. The director finally selected one and handed it to him.

It was headed *Low Level Project*, and a glance told Alan it was the proposed plan to seal off the lower levels from the upper ones.

So Helen had been right in her thinking. Simon Powys did

25

hold sufficient sway with the City Council to have his 'suggestions' put into action.

Carson was staring at his own right thumb. He did not look up. "It will involve temporarily re-routing pedestrian traffic, of course, though to save trouble we could work at night. It would be worth paying the men double overtime to get it done as quickly as possible."

"With a minimum of fuss?" Alan said with an edge to his voice.

"Exactly."

"The Council hasn't announced this publicly, I presume?"

"There's no need to—no one lives in the lower levels any more. There will be emergency doors constructed, naturally, but these will be kept locked. It shouldn't bother anyone . . ."

"Except the Fireclown!" Alan was so furious that he found difficulty in controlling himself.

"Ah, yes. The Fireclown. I expect he'll find somewhere else to go. Probably he'll leave the City altogether. I suspect he's no real right to live there in the first place."

"But the newspapers, the laservid, the RLM—and therefore the main weight of public opinion—all regard the Fireclown in a favourable way. He has a good part of the world on his side. This isn't political dynamite—it's a political megabang!"

"Quite." Carson nodded, still regarding his thumb. "But we aren't concerned with politics, are we, Alan? This is just another job for us—a simple one. Let's get it over with."

Alan took the papers Carson handed him and got up. The director was right, but he could not help feeling personally involved.

"I'll get started after lunch," he promised. He went back to his office, put the papers in his confidential drawer, went to the roof of the C.A. building and took a cab across the spacious artificial countryside of the Top towards his grandfather's apartments, which lay close to the Solar House at South Top.

But when he got there he found only Junnar and another of his cousins—Helen's brother, Denholm Curtis.

Curtis dressed with challenging bad taste. His clothes were a deliberate attack, a weapon which he flaunted. They proclaimed him an iconoclast impatient of any accepted dogma whether reasonable or not. Above the striped and polka-dotted trappings draping his lean body was a firm, sensitive head— the heavy Powys head with calm eyes, hopeful, seeming to be

26

aware of detail and yet disdainful of it. Curtis's eyes were fixed on the future.

"Hello, Denholm, how are you?" He and his cousin shook hands.

"Fine—and you?"

"Not bad. And how's the Thirty Five Group? Still bent on gingering up the mother party?"

Curtis led the radical wing of the Solref party. His group was small but vociferous and carried a certain amount of weight in the Solar House. Yet, though they stuck to the traditional party of the Powys family, he would have been much more at home in his sister's movement. But his interest was in changing the party to change the policy rather than splitting away from it and forming a fresh one.

Curtis hadn't replied to Alan's question. He glanced at the big wall-clock just as his grandfather came hurrying in through the side door.

"Grandfather." Alan stepped quickly forward but old Simon Powys shook his head.

"Sorry, Alan. I have to get to the Solar House immediately. Coming, Denholm?"

Curtis nodded and the two of them left the room almost at a run.

Something was in the air, Alan guessed, and it wasn't the closing down of the lower levels. This seemed much more important.

"What's going on, Junnar?"

The Negro looked slightly embarrassed as their eyes met, but he spoke coolly.

"They're calling on old Benjosef to resign."

Benjosef, a dedicated member of the Solrefs, was Solar President. His two terms of office had been popular but not particularly enlightened. He had not had much public support over the last year, partly because he was slow to agree on a policy of expansion and colonization involving Mars and Ganymede.

"On what issue?"

"The planets. Ganymede and Mars are ready for settlers. There are businessmen willing to invest in them, ships ready to take them—but Benjosef is reluctant to pursue a policy of expansion because *he* says we haven't a sufficiently good organization for controlling it yet. He wants to wait another ten

27

years to build up such an organization, but everyone else is impatient to get started. You know the story . . ."

"I know it," Alan agreed.

The projects to make the two planets inhabitable and fertile had been started over a hundred years previously and it had been hard enough holding private enterprise and would-be settlers back before they were ready. Benjosef had been foolish to take a stand on the issue, but he had done what he thought was right and his conviction now seemed likely to topple him.

"What are his chances of staying in power for the rest of his term?" Alan asked curiously.

"Bad. Minister Powys and the majority of Solrefs have to stand by him, of course, but Mr. Curtis and his group have sided with the RLMs. The other parties are fairly equally divided between both sides, but Mr. Curtis's support should give the vote against the President."

Once again Alan was glad he had decided to have no part of politics. Even his just and stern old grandfather was going to behave like a hypocrite, giving a vote of confidence for Benjosef while encouraging Curtis to vote against him.

He decided that there wasn't much he could do, since everyone would be at the Solar House, including, of course, Helen. The current session ended in a fortnight and the next President would have to be elected during the recession. Probably, he thought ironically, both the main runners had their machines all geared for action.

"You'll be kept pretty busy from now on, I should think," he said to Junnar. The Negro nodded, and Alan continued: "What were you doing in the lower levels last night?"

"Keeping an eye on the Fireclown," Junnar said shortly.

"For grandfather?"

"Yes, of course."

"Why is he so malevolent toward the Fireclown? He seems harmless to me. Has grandfather any special knowledge that the public doesn't have?" Alan was only partly interested in what he himself was saying. The other half of his mind was wondering about the elections—and Helen.

Junnar shook his head. "I don't think so. It's a question of your point of view. Minister Powys sees the Fireclown as a threat to society and its progress. Others simply see him as a romantic figure who wants a return to a simpler life. That's why he's such a popular cause with so many people. We all

28

wish life were simpler—we're suckers for the kind of simple answer to our problems that a man like the Fireclown supplies."

"Simple answers, sure enough," Alan nodded, "but hardly realistic."

"Who knows?" Junnar said tersely.

"Is grandfather going to use the Fireclown as a platform?"

"I expect so. It will be taken for granted that whoever wins will encourage the expansion bill. So the other main dispute will be the Fireclown."

"But it's out of all proportion. Why should the Fireclown become a major issue?"

Junnar smiled cynically. "Probably because the politicians want him to be."

That answer satisfied Alan and he added:

"Hitler, as I remember, used the Jews. Before him, Nero used the Christians. Minority groups are always useful—they turn people's attention away from real issues which the politicians have no control over. So Miss Curtis and Minister Powys are using the Fireclown, is that it? One in support, one against. People will take an interest in a battle over such a colourful figure and forget to question other policies. It sounds almost unbelievable, yet it happens. History proves that. What does grandfather plan to do about the Fireclown if he gets to power?"

"Maybe nothing," Junnar said. "Maybe nothing at all—once he's in power." Then he smiled brightly. "No, it's not fair. After all, I am Simon Powys's private secretary. He really is deeply concerned about what the Fireclown represents rather than the man himself."

The apparent return of loyalty in Junnar brought an awakening echo in Alan. He nodded.

"Perhaps we don't do either of them justice. I was forgetting they are both Powyses with a strong sense of family honour."

Junnar coughed. "I think I'd better go over to the Solar House myself. Can I arrange an appointment for you to see your grandfather?"

"No, don't bother."

"Are you going to the Fireclown's audience tomorrow?"

"Probably."

"I may see you there."

"Yes," said Alan. He glanced at his watch and noted that he would arrive back to his office late. He and Junnar walked into the corridor and went their separate ways.

Alan sighed as he studied the Low Level project. Basically it was a simple job to organize the sealing off of all entrances, stopping elevators and escalators and cutting off light and heating where they existed. Ten levels were to be shut down, involving the moving of less than a thousand people to accommodation higher up. The residents of levels nine and ten would welcome the change, he knew. They, at least, could be relied upon to support the operation.

No, it wasn't the project itself but the way the newspapers and entertainment media would treat it, what Helen Curtis would say about it. It was going to cause City Administration and the City Council as much trouble as if they told the populace they had decided to torture and kill all pet dogs in the City. And this move would have world-wide repercussions—the Fireclown had been the subject of innumerable popular features treating him in a sympathetic manner.

Already he was convinced that his grandfather had committed political suicide by this move. But, for the moment, he wasn't worried so much about that as about the trouble he and the director would come in for.

He, in particular, would be slandered—the grandson of the man who wanted to victimize the innocent Fireclown. He would be talked of as a puppet in the hands of the old man. Doubtless he would even be shouted at in the public corridors.

He contacted City Works, waited for the manager to be located.

Tristran B'Ula was, like Junnar, a Zimbabwean from what had once been Rhodesia. The State of Zimbabwe had grown to great power in the African Federation and many of the Solar System's best administrators came from there.

"Good afternoon, Tristran." Alan was on friendly terms with the manager. "New project I'd like to have a word with you about."

B'Ula pretended to groan. "Is it important? All my available manpower is taken up at the moment."

"The City Council wants us to give this priority. It's also highly confidential. Is there anyone else in the room with you?"

B'Ula turned, looked behind him and said: "Would you

mind leaving the room for a minute or two, Miss Nagib?"

His pretty Egyptian secretary crossed the screen.

"Okay, Alan. What is it?"

"City Council wants us to seal off ten levels—numbers one to ten, to be precise. Concrete in the entrances, lighting, heat and water supply cut off, elevators and escalators to stop operation."

It took B'Ula a moment to absorb all this. His face showed incredulity. "But that's where the Fireclown is! What are we expected to do? Wall him up—entomb him?"

"Of course not. All residents will be moved before the project goes ahead. I'd thought of housing them in those spare corridors in Section Six of the Fifteenth Level and Sections Twelve and Thirteen of the Seventeenth Level. They'll need to be checked to make sure they're perfectly habitable. The Chemical Research Institute were going to take them over since they're getting a bit cramped, but they'll have to. . ."

"Just a minute. Alan. What's going to happen to the Fireclown?"

"Presumably, he'll take the alternative accommodation we're offering to everyone else," Alan said grimly.

"You know he wouldn't do that!"

"I don't know the Fireclown."

"Well, I'm having no part of it," B'Ula said rebelliously, then he switched out.

Completely taken aback, Alan sat at his desk breathing heavily. This, he decided, was only a hint of how the news would be received by the public. His colleague had always struck him as a solid, practical man who did his job well—a good civil servant, like himself. If Tristan B'Ula could be so affected by the news as to risk his position by refusing to obey the City Council, then how would others take it?

The word *Riot* popped into Alan's head. There had been no public disorder in a hundred years!

This was even bigger than he'd expected.

Another thing—B'Ula felt so strongly about it that he wasn't likely to keep the project secret. Someone had to convince the Zimbabwean that the closing off of the levels was not a threat against the Fireclown. Reluctantly, he would have to tell Carson of his little scene with the manager.

Slowly he got up from his desk. Slowly he walked into Carson's office.

CHAPTER FOUR

BENJOSEF had resigned.

After a meeting in the Solar House lasting well into the night as Benjosef tried to put his arguments to the Solar representatives, the old President had been shouted down.

Denholm Curtis had asked for a vote of no confidence in Benjosef. The ballot had been secret, and though Simon Powys had seemed to support Benjosef it had been a masterly deception. He had managed to convey the image of a strong man standing beside his leader out of nothing but loyalty. In spite of favouring—or appearing to favour—Benjosef's cautious policies, Simon Powys had risen in public esteem. Doubtless the heavy Solref vote would be his in the election. Alan was sure that his grandfather had actually voted again Benjosef. Principles the old man might have—and plenty of them—but they seemed at that moment to carry little weight against Simon Powys's actions. This strange duality which seemed to come upon even the best politicians was not new to Alan, yet it constantly shocked him.

At 0200 Benjosef, baffled by what he considered mad recklessness on the part of the Solar House, reluctantly resigned as President, his term of office, which should have continued for another eighteen months, to finish with the current session.

Alan read and saw all this as he breakfasted, glancing from news-sheet to laservid and constructing all the details of the dramatic, and in some ways tragic, session. He rather sympathized with Benjosef. Perhaps he was old and wise, perhaps he was just old. Simon Powys was only five years younger, but he possessed a forceful vitality that belied his age. Alan observed, judiciously, that Helen Curtis had not actually demanded the President's resignation, though other members of her party had been vociferous in attacking him. It would not have been diplomatic or polite for a would-be President to ask the current head to step down.

He sighed and finished his coffee—a new brand from which the caffeine had been removed and replaced by a stimulant described as 'less harmful'. The strange thing was it tasted better, though he would have liked to have denied this.

So now the fight was between his grandfather and his cousin. Would Simon Powys see the light of day at last and ignore the Fireclown issue? As yet, of course, it had not really become an issue. It would take a political battle to make it one. Or would he plug on? Alan had a sad feeling that he would—particularly if Helen drew the Fireclown into her platform.

When he got to the office Carson was looking pale and even less savoury than usual. People were not chosen as directors of City Administration for their looks; but at this moment Alan rather wished they had a smiling, pleasant-faced he-man who could cozen the public into realizing the truth of the situation.

"What did B'Ula have to say, sir?" Alan asked.

"I was unable to contact him, Alan. I tried the Works but he must have left immediately he switched out on you. I tried his private number but his wife said he had not come back. When I tried again later he still wasn't there."

"What was he doing, I wonder?"

"I can tell you. He was broadcasting the news everywhere. Not only broadcasting but elaborating it. You can imagine what he said."

"I can imagine what would be said by some. But B'Ula . . ."

"I've just had Chairman Fou on the line. He says the Council is most disturbed, thinks we should have been able to judge B'Ula better. I pointed out, somewhat obscurely, that they appointed B'Ula. But it seems we're the scapegoats—from the public's point of view and evidently from the Council's."

"The news this morning was so full of 'stormy scenes in the Solar House' that they probably haven't got round to us yet," Alan said with mock cheerfulness. "But doubtless we'll be getting it in an hour or two."

"I expect so. Well, we've still got work to do. I'm going over to Works myself, to see what the men think of the project. If they oppose it as strongly as B'Ula we're going to have trouble with the unions before long."

"What will we do if that happens?"

"Brick up the bloody levels ourselves, I suppose." Carson swore.

"Black labour!" Alan said, shocked. "We'd have a system-wide strike on our hands then!" It was true.

"I'm hoping the City Council will realize the implications and back down gracefully." Carson walked towards the door. "But they didn't seem as if they were going to, judging by

Chairman Fou's tone. Goodbye, Alan. Better stick to something routine until I find out what's happening."

When Alan buzzed for his filing clerk his secretary came in. He raised an eyebrow. "Where's Levy?"

"He didn't come in this morning, Mr. Powys."

"Is he sick?"

"I don't think so. I heard a rumour he'd asked for his back pay from the cashiers and said something about resigning."

"I see. Then will you bring me the Pedestrian Transport file? Number PV12, I think it is."

As he ploughed through the monotonous work, Alan learned from his secretary that about a quarter of the staff in the C.A. building had not turned up for work that morning. That represented over three hundred people. Where were they all? It was evident why they had left.

The whole business was growing into a monster. If three hundred people from one building alone could feel so strongly about the Fireclown, how many millions were there supporting him?

To Alan it was incredible. He knew, intuitively, that so many people could not be roused merely because of the proposed closing down of ten virtually unused levels—or, for that matter, give up their jobs in support of the Fireclown. It must be that the Fireclown represented something, some need in modern mankind which, perhaps, the sociologists would know about. He decided not to ask a sociologist and risk being plied with so many explanatory theories that his mind would be still further confused.

But what was this tenuous *zeitgeist?*

Perhaps the world would be in flames before he ever found out. Perhaps, whatever happened, no one would ever really know. He decided he was being too melodramatic. On the other hand, he was extremely disturbed. He had a liking for peace and quiet—one of the reasons why he had rejected the idea of entering politics—and the world's mood was distinctly unpeaceful.

Facing facts, he realized that this was not a localized outbreak, that it would have to grow in magnitude before it died down or was controlled. What had his grandfather started? Nothing, really of course. His move had merely served to bring it out into the open, whatever it was.

But the people's hysteria was increasing, becoming evident

34

everywhere. An hysteria that had not entered the human race since the war scares two centuries earlier. It seemed to have blown up overnight, though perhaps he had seen its beginnings in the worship of the Fireclown, the demand for Benjosef's resignation and other, smaller, incidents that he had not recognized for what they were.

The morning dragged. In the back of his mind something else nagged him until he realized that this was the night when the Fireclown was to hold his 'audience'. He felt slightly perturbed at attending it now that public anger seemed to be building to such a pitch, but he had said he would go, promised himself that he would go—and he would.

Carson came back just as Alan's secretary brought him some lunch.

"Any luck?" Alan said, offering his boss a slice of bread impregnated with beef extract. Carson refused it with an irritable wave of his hand, apologizing for his brusque gesture with a slight smile.

"None. Most of the workmen didn't turn up this morning, anyway. The union leaders deny influencing them, but someone has ..."

"B'Ula?"

"Yes. He spoke to a public meeting last night, attended by most of the men who work for him. Told them that this victimization of the simple Fireclown was a threat also to *their* liberty. The usual stuff. And once the news got round, he wasn't the only one talking and rabble-rousing. At least a dozen others have used the same theme in speeches to incredibly big crowds. They didn't have to do much convincing, either. The crowds were already on their side."

"It's all happened so suddenly." Alan repeated his earlier thoughts aloud. "You wouldn't think a thing like this could grow so fast. People aren't even bothering to speak to their political representatives or beam the City Council."

"That's what's so peculiar. We might have expected angry letters demanding that we call a halt to the project—and if we'd had enough of them we should have had to. That's democracy, after all. I'd really thought the idea of law and order had finally sunk into the human race. Looks as if I was wrong."

"Disproves the Fireclown's cant about 'artificial living' producing 'artificial' men and ideas. The public's chock-a-block

35

with human nature this morning. They seem as hysterical and as bloodthirsty as they ever were."

"Mass neurosis and all that." Carson stared at his thumb, inspecting the nail. It was dirty. However much he cleaned them his nails always seemed to get dirty a few moments afterwards.

By mid-afternoon, Carson and Alan were staring in blank incredulity at one another. At least two hundred more people had not come back after lunch. It was useless to attempt continuing work.

Another disturbing point was that they had been unable to contact the City Council. The beam had been jammed continuously. Obviously *some* people had decided to ask the City Council about the matter.

"I think we'd better go quietly to our homes," Carson said with a worried attempt at jocularity. "I'll keep a skeleton staff on and give the rest the afternoon off. I might as well, they'll probably be walking out soon, anyway."

Glad of this for his own reasons, Alan agreed.

He returned to his flat and changed into the nondescript suit he had worn earlier. He had had some trouble getting there, for the corridors were packed. Angry and excited conversations were going on all over the place. Ordered discipline had given way to disorganized hysteria and it rather frightened him to see ordinary human beings behaving in a manner which, to him, was a rejection of their better selves.

Outside in the jostling corridor he was carried by the crowd to the elevators and had to wait for nearly a quarter of an hour as the mob's impatience grew. There just weren't enough elevators to take them all at once.

Down, down, down the levels. Into level nine and they milled down the escalators and ramps, Alan unable to go back now even if he had wanted to.

The smoke from the torches of the first level, the smell of sweat, the atmosphere of tension, the ululating roar of the crowd all attacked his senses and threatened to drug his brain as the crowd entered a huge cavern which, he knew, had once been part of an underground airstrip during the years when the City had first been planned.

And at last he saw the Fireclown, standing upon the tall column that served him as a dais, seeming to balance his huge bulk precariously on the platform.

There above him, Alan saw the spluttering mass of the artificial sun. He remembered having heard of it. The Fireclown had made it—or had it made—and somehow controlled it.

"What's this? What's this?" The Fireclown was shouting. "Why so many? Has the whole world suddenly seen the error of its ways?"

There were affirmative shouts from all around him as the crowd answered, somewhat presumptuously, for the rest of the planet's millions.

The Fireclown laughed, his gross bulk wobbling on the dais.

Thousands upon thousands of people were packing into the cavern, threatening to crush those already at the centre. Alan found himself borne towards the dais as the Fireclown's reverberating laugh swept over them.

"No more!" the Fireclown cried suddenly. "Corso—tell them they can't come in . . . Tell them to come back later. We'll be suffocated!"

The Fireclown seemed baffled by the crowd's size—bewildered, perhaps, by his own power.

Yet was it his own power? Alan wondered. Was not the mob identifying the Fireclown with something else, some deep-rooted need in them which was finding expression through the Clown?

But it was immaterial to speculate. The fact remained that the Fireclown had become the mob's symbol and its leader. Whatever he told them they would do—unless, perhaps, he told them to do nothing at all.

The mob was beginning to chant:

"Fireclown! Fireclown! Fireclown! Speak to us!"

"How shall the world end?" he cried.

"In fire! In fire!"

"How shall it be born again?"

"In fire!"

"And the fire shall be the fire of man's spirit!" the Fireclown roared. "The fire in his brain and his belly. Too long has the world lived on artificial nourishment. The nourishment of processed food, the nourishment of words that have no relation to reality, the nourishment of ideas that exist in a vacuum. We are losing our birthright! Our heritage faces extinction!"

He paused as the mob moved like a mighty, restless tide. Then he continued:

"I am your phoenix, awash with the flames of life! I am

your salvation! You see flames above." He raised an orange-painted hand to the spluttering orb near the ceiling of the cavern. "You see flames around you." He indicated the torches. "But these fires only represent the real flames, the unseen flames which exist within you, and the Mother of Life which sweeps the heavens above you—the Sun!"

"The Sun!" the mob shrieked.

"Yes, the Sun! Billions of years ago our planet was formed from the stuff of the Sun. The Sun nurtured life, and it finally nurtured the life of our earliest ancestors. It has nurtured us since. But does modern man honour his mother?"

"No! No!"

"No! Our ancestors worshipped the Sun for millennia! Why? Because they recognized it as the Mother of Life. Without the Sun man could never have been born on Earth! The Earth itself could not have been formed!"

Some of the mob, obviously old hands at this, shouted: "Fire is Life!"

"Yes," the Fireclown roared. "Fire is Life. And how many of you here have ever seen the Sun? How many of you have ever been warmed directly by its rays? How many of you have ever seen a naked flame?"

A wordless bellow greeted each question.

Alan had to fight the infectious hysteria of the crowd. Though it was true that many of the City's populace had never been outside, they had led better and fuller lives within the walls. And there was nothing forbidding them to take a vacation beyond the City. It was a kind of agoraphobia, not the State, which held them back. They had, at any rate, reaped the benefits of the Sun in less direct ways—from the great solar batteries which supplied power to the City.

As if he anticipated these unspoken thoughts, the Fireclown carried on:

"We are misusing the Sun. We are perverting the stuff of life and changing it to the stuff of death! We use the Sun to power our machines and keep us alive in plastic, metal and concrete coffins. We use the Sun to push our spaceships to the planets —planets where we are forced to live in wholly artificial conditions, or planets which we warp and change from what they naturally are into planets that copy Earth. That is wrong! Who are we to change the natural order? We are playing literally with fire—and that fire will soon turn and shrivel us!"

"Yes! Yes!"

In an effort to remain out of the Fireclown's spell, Alan encouraged himself to feel dubiously towards the logic of what he was saying. He continued in that vein for some time, drumming the words into the ready ears of the mob, again and again.

The Fireclown's argument wasn't new. It had been said, in milder ways, by philosophers and politicians of a certain bent for centuries—possibly since the birth of the industrial revolution. But, for all this, the argument wasn't necessarily right. It came back to the question of whether it was better for man to be an unenlightened savage in the caves, or whether he should use the reasoning powers and the powers of invention which were his in order to gain knowledge.

Feeling as if he had hit upon an inkling of the trouble, Alan realized that the Fireclown and those, like his grandfather, who opposed him were both only supporting opinions. Any forthcoming dispute was likely to be a battle between ignorance of one sort and ignorance of another.

Yet the fact remained—trouble was brewing. Big trouble unless something could be done about it.

"All religions have seen the Sun as a representation of God . . ." the Fireclown was saying now.

Perhaps he was sincere, Alan thought; perhaps he was innocent of personal ambition, unaware of the furore he was likely to create, thoughtless of the conflict that was likely to ensue.

And yet Alan was attracted to the Fireclown. He *liked* him and took a delight in the man's vitality and spontaneity. It was merely unfortunate that he should have come at a time when public neurosis had reached such a peak.

Now a voice was shouting something about the City Council. Fragmented phrases reached Alan about the closing of the levels, an attack against the Fireclown, a threat to free speech. It was marvellous how they accepted the principles of democracy and rejected them at the same time by talk of mob action!

Marvellous—and deeply frightening. He turned to see if he could get back and out. He could not. The mob pressed closer, packed itself tighter. A horrifying vision of thousands of mouthing faces surrounded him. He panicked momentarily and then suppressed his panic. It could not help him. Little could.

The Fireclown's voice bellowed for silence, swore at the mob, reviled it. Abashed, the crowd quieted.

"You see! You see! This is what you do. So the City Council is to close off the levels. Perhaps it is because of me, perhaps it isn't! But does it matter?"

Certain elements shouted that it did matter.

"What kind of threat am I to the City Council? What threat am I to anyone? I tell you—none!"

Alan was mystified by these words, just as the mob was.

"None! I want no part of your demonstrations, your petty fears and puny conflicts! I do not expect action from you. I do not want action. I want you only to become aware! You can change your physical environment, certainly. But first you must change your mental attitude. Study the words you are using today. Study them and you will find them meaningless. You have emotions—you have words. But the words you have do not describe your emotions. Try to think of words that will! Then you will be strong. Then you will have no need for your stupid, overvaunted so-called 'intelligence'. Then you will have no need to march against the Council Building!"

Alan himself sought for words to describe the Fireclown's state at that moment. What had been said had impressed him in spite of his decision to observe as objectively as possible. They meant nothing much, really. They had been said before. But they hinted at something—gave him a clue . . .

Noble bewilderment. The elephant attacked by small boys. And yet concerned for them. Alan was impressed by what he felt to be the Fireclown's intrinsic innocence. But such an innocence, it could topple the world!

Placards now began to appear in the crowd:

NO TO BURYING THE FIRECLOWN!

HANDS OFF THE LOWER LEVELS!

COUNCIL CAN'T QUENCH THE FIRE OF MAN!

Amused by the ludicrous messages, Alan made out others. SONS OF THE SUN REJECT COUNCIL PLAN! was, perhaps, the best.

His mind began to skip, taking in first a fragmented scene —faces, placards, turbulent movement, a woman's ecstatic face; then a clipping of sound, a sudden idea that he could easily follow the Fireclown if he could hear the man convince him in cooler, more intellectual phrases; the flaring gash of light that quickly bubbled from the tiny sun and then seemed to be drawn back into it.

"Fools!" The Fireclown was shouting, incredulity and anger mixed on his painted face.

It seemed to Alan that the paint had been stripped away and, for the first time, he became aware of the *man* who stood there. An individual, complex and enigmatic.

But the glimpse did not last, for he felt the pressure from behind decreasing.

At least half the mob had turned away and were surging towards the cavern's exit.

And the Fireclown? Alan looked up. The Fireclown was appealing to them to stay, but his words were drowned by the babble of hysteria.

Now Alan was borne back with the crowd, was forced to turn and move with it or risk being trampled. He looked up at the dais and saw that the fat body of the Fireclown had developed a slump that hardly seemed in keeping with his earlier vitality.

As the mob boiled up to the third level, Alan saw Helen Curtis only a few yards ahead of him and to his left. He kept her in sight and managed, gradually, to inch through the stabbing elbows and hard shoulders.

On the ninth level he was just able to get into the same elevator with her. He shouted over the heads of the others:

"Helen! What the hell are you doing here?"

He saw a placard, FIRECLOWN FIRST VICTIM OF DICTATORSHIP, bob up and down and realized she was holding it.

"Do you think this will win you votes?" he demanded.

She made no reply but smiled at him. "I'm glad to see you came. Are you with us?"

"No, I'm not. And I don't think the Fireclown is either! He doesn't want you to fight for his 'rights'—I'm sure he's perfectly able to look after himself!"

"It's the principle!"

"Rubbish!"

The doors of the giant elevator slid up and they crossed the corridor to the row of elevators opposite. The liveried attendants attempted to hold the crowd away but were pushed back into their own elevators by the force of the rush. He managed to catch up with her and stood with his body tight against her side, unable to shift his position.

"This sort of thing may win you immediate popularity with the rabble, but what are the responsible voters going to think?"

"I'm fighting for what I think right," she said defiantly, grimly.

"You're fighting . . ." He shook his head. "Look, when we reach Sixty Five make your way home. Speak for the Fire-clown in the Solar House if you must, but don't make a fool of yourself. When this hysteria dies down you'll look ridiculous."

"So you think this is going to die down?" she said sweetly.

The doors opened, the elevators disgorged their contents and they were on the move again, streaming across the quiet gardens towards the distant Civic Buildings.

It was night. The sky beyond the dome was dark. The crowd exhibited a moment's nervous and calm, its pace slowed and then, as Helen shouted: "There! That's where they are!" and flung her hand theatrically towards the Council Building, they moved on again, spreading out and running.

Laservid cameramen and still-photographers were waiting for them, taking pictures as they surged past.

Helen began to run awkwardly, her placard waving in her hands.

Let her go, Alan thought, old emotions returning to heighten his confusion. He turned back.

No! She mustn't do it! He hated her political ambitions, but they meant much to her. She could throw everything away with this ill-considered action of hers.

Or would she? Perhaps the day of ordered government was already over.

"Helen!" He ran after her, tripped and fell heavily on a bed of trampled blue roses, got up. "Helen!"

He couldn't see her. Ahead of the crowd lights were going on in the Civic Buildings. Fortuitously, and perhaps happily for the City Council—all of whom had private apartments in the Council Building—the headquarters of the City Police were only a block away. And that building was lit up also.

He hoped the police would use restraint in dealing with the crowd.

When he finally saw Helen again she was leading the van

of the mob who now chanted the unoriginal phrase: "We want the Council!"

Unarmed policemen in their blue smocks and broad belts began to muscle their way through the crowd. Laservid cameras tracked them.

Alan grasped Helen's arm, trying to make himself heard above the chant. "Helen! For God's sake get out—you're liable to be arrested. The police are here!"

"So what?" Her face was flushed, her eyes over-bright, her voice high.

He reached up and tore the placard from her hands, flinging it to the ground. "I don't want to see you ruined!"

She stood there, her body taut with anger, staring into his face. "You always were jealous of my political success!"

"Can't you see what's happening to you? If you must play follow-my-leader, do it in a more orderly way. You could be President soon."

"And I still will be. Go away!"

He shook her shoulders. "Open your eyes! Open your eyes!"

"Oh don't be so melodramatic. Leave me alone. My eyes are wide open!"

But he could see she had softened slightly, perhaps simply because of the interest he was taking in her.

Then a voice blared: "Go back to your homes! If you have any complaints, lodge them in the proper manner. The Council provide facilities for hearing complaints. This demonstration will get you nowhere! The police are authorized to stop anyone attempting to enter the Council Building!"

Helen listened until the broadcast finished. Then she shouted: "Don't let them put you off! They'll do nothing until they see we mean business."

Two hundred years of peace had taught Helen Curtis nothing about peaceful demonstration.

It was such a small issue, Alan told himself bewilderedly, such a small issue that could have been settled by a hundred angry letters instead of a mob of thousands.

The crowd was attempting to press past the police barrier.

Finally the barrier broke and fights between the police and the demonstrators broke out. Several times Alan saw a policeman lose his temper and strike a demonstrator.

He was disgusted and perturbed, but there was nothing he could do.

43

Wearily, he walked away from the scene. For the time being all emotion had been driven from him.

CHAPTER FIVE

MISERABLY, unsure of his direction, Alan let his feet carry him aimlessly.

He was sure that the riot marked some important change in the course of Earth's history, but knew with equal certainty that it would be twenty years before he could look back and judge why it had happened.

Helen, I love you, he thought, *Helen I love you*. But it was no good. They were completely separated now. He had picked an old scab. He should have left it well alone.

He looked up and found that he was approaching the building which housed his grandfather's apartment. He realized at the same time that he needed someone to talk to. There had been no one since he and Helen had parted. The stern old man would probably refuse to listen and would almost certainly refuse to give him any advice or help, but there was nothing else for it.

He did not have a sonarkey for the matterlift, so he climbed the stairs very slowly and went to the main door of the big apartment.

A servant answered and showed him in.

Simon Powys was sitting in his lounge intently watching the laservid relaying scenes of the riots outside. He turned his great head and Alan saw that his brooding eyes held a hint of triumph.

"So the Fireclown was uninterested in power, was he?" Simon Powys smiled slightly and pointed at the set. "Then what's that, Alan?"

"A riot," Alan said hollowly. "But though it's in the name of the Fireclown he didn't encourage it."

"That seems unlikely. You were mixed up in it for a while, weren't you? I saw you on that"—he pointed again at the screen. "And Helen, too, is taking an active part."

"Very active," Alan kept his tone dry.

"You disapprove?"

"I tried to stop her."

"So you've changed your opinion of the Fireclown. You realize I was right. If I had my way, every one of those rioters would be flung into prison—and the Fireclown exiled from the planet!"

Slightly shocked by the savagery of his grandfather's last remark, Alan remained silent. Together they watched the laservid. The police seemed to be coping, though their numbers had had to be increased.

"I haven't changed my opinion, grandfather," he said quietly. "Not really, anyway."

His grandfather also paused before replying: "I wish you knew what I knew—then you'd fight the Fireclown as strongly as I'm attempting to. The man's a criminal. Perhaps he's more than that. Perhaps this is the last night we'll be able to sit comfortably and watch the laservid."

"We both seemed to underestimate the Fireclown's popularity," Alan mused. "Are you going to continue your campaign against him?"

"Of course."

"I should have thought you would spend your time better trying to find out *why* the public is attracted to him?"

"The Fireclown's a menace ..."

"Why?" Alan said grimly.

"Because he threatens the stability of society. We've had equilibrium for two hundred years ..."

"*Why* does he threaten the stability of society?"

Simon Powys turned round in his chair. "Are you trying to be impertinent, Alan?"

"I'm trying to tell you that the Fireclown himself means nothing. The public is in this mood for another, a deeper, reason. I was down there in the cavern on the first level. I saw the Fireclown try to stop them from doing this but they wouldn't listen to him. Why?"

But the old man stubbornly refused to get drawn into an argument. And Alan felt a hollow sense of frustration. His urge to try to clarify his thoughts by means of conversation was unbearably strong. He tried again:

"Grandfather!"

"Yes?"

"The Fireclown pleaded with the crowd not to make this demonstration. I saw him. But the crowd wasn't interested in what he said. They're using him, just as you and Helen are using him for your own reasons. There is something deeper going on. Can't you see that?"

Again the old man looked up at him. "Very well. The Fire-clown symbolizes something—something wrong in our society, is that it? If that's the case we cannot strike at the general, we must strike at the particular, because that is what is tangible. I am striking at the Fireclown."

Alan wasn't satisfied. His grandfather's words were reason-able, yet he suspected that no thought or sensibility lay behind them. His answer had been too pat.

"I intend to do everything possible to bring the Fireclown's activities to a halt," Simon Powys continued. "The public may be too blind to see what is happening to them, what dangerous power the Clown wields over them, but I will make them see. I will make them see!"

Alan shrugged. It seemed to him that the blind were accus-ing the blind.

"Politicians!" he said, suddenly angry. "What hollow indi-viduals they are!"

Suddenly, his grandfather rose in his chair and got up, his back to the laservid, his face taut with suppressed emotion.

"By God, I brought you up as a Powys in spite of your mother's shaming me. I recognized you. I refused to take the easy way out and pay some woman to call you her own. You received the name of Powys and the benefits of that name. And this is how you reward me, by coming to my own house and insulting me! I fostered a bastard—and now that bastard re-verts to type! You have never understood the responsibilities and the need to serve which marks our family. We are not power-seekers, we aren't meddlers in the affairs of others! We are dedicated to furthering civilization and humanity through-out the Solar System! What do you understand of that, Alan whatever-your-name-is?"

"I think it most noble," Alan sneered, trying to hold back the tears of pain and anger in his eyes. His body trembled as it had done when, as an adolescent, he had been told the story of his birth. "Most noble, grandfather, all you and the Powys clan have done for me! But you could not keep my mother alive with your high sentiments! You would not let her marry the man who fathered me! I know that much from grand-mother. Some rough spaceman, wasn't it? Could you kill him by shame, the way you killed my mother?"

46

"Your mother killed herself. I did everything for her . . ."

"And judged her for everything!"

"No . . ." The old man's face softened.

"I've always given you the benefit of every doubt, grandfather. I've always respected you. But in this business of the Fireclown I've seen that you can be unreasoningly dogmatic, that perhaps what I've heard about you was true! Your attack on me was unfair—just as your attack on the Fireclown is unfair!"

"If you knew, Alan. If you knew just what . . ." The old man straightened his back. "I apologize for what I said to you. I'm tired—busy day—not thinking properly. I'll see you tomorrow, perhaps."

Alan nodded wordlessly and left, moved to an emotion towards his grandfather which, he decided, could only be love. Love? After what they had both said? It seemed to him that everything was turning upside down. The chaos of the mob, the chaos of his own moods, the chaos of his private life—all seemed to point towards something. Some remedy, perhaps, for his own and the world's ills?

On the roof of the building he looked around for a car which would carry him above the riot below to North Top, where he could probably use one of the small private elevators. Above the dome the sky was clear and the moon rode the sky in a casual arc. Near the edge of the roof he saw Junnar.

The Zimbabwean was also watching the distant rioters.

"You're too late," he said cheerfully. "You missed the best of it. They're dispersing now."

"I was *in* the best of it." Alan joined him and saw that a much smaller crowd continued to demonstrate, but that most of the people were moving slowly back towards the elevator-cone.

"Did you see any arrests?" Junnar asked.

"No. Did you?"

"The police didn't seem too keen. I think they took a couple in—probably examples."

"What does all this mean, Junnar? What's happening to the world?"

"I'm not with you?" Junnar stared at Alan in curiosity.

"Nobody is, I guess. I'm sure that these riots are not just the result of the Fireclown's speeches in his cavern. I'm sure

47

they've been brewing for ages. Why are the people so frustrated they have to break out like this suddenly? What do they want? What do they lack? You may know as well as I do that mass demonstrations in the past were often nothing to do with the placards they waved and the cant they chanted—it was some universal need crying out for satisfaction, something that has always been in man, however happy and comfortable his world is. What is it this time?"

"I think I know what you mean." Junnar offered Alan a marijuana but he refused. "That down there—the Fireclown —the impatience to expand to the new Earth-type planets— the bitter arguments in the Solar House—individual frustration —the 'time for a change' leaders in the news-sheets and laservid programmes. All threatening to topple society from its carefully maintained equilibrium. You mean it's some kind of"— Junnar groped for a word—"*force* that's entered the race, that we should be doing something, changing our direction in some way?"

"I think that's roughly what I mean. I'm finding it hard to put it into words myself."

"Well, this is perhaps what the Fireclown means when he says we're turning our backs on the natural life. With all our material comfort, perhaps we should look inward at ourselves instead of looking outward at the new colony planets. Well, what do we do about it, Mr. Powys?"

"I wish I knew."

"So do I." Junnar exhaled the sweet smoke and leaned back against the rail.

"You seem to understand what the Fireclown's getting at. *You* must believe that he's innocent of causing these riots. Can't you tell my grandfather that?"

Junnar's manner changed. "I didn't say the Fireclown was innocent, Mr. Powys. I agree with your grandfather. He's a menace!" He spoke fiercely, almost as fiercely as Simon Powys had done earlier.

Alan sighed. "Oh, all right. Goodnight, Junnar."

"'Night, Mr. Powys."

As he climbed into an automatic car and set the control, he caught a final glimpse of the Negro's sad face staring up at the moon like a dog about to bay.

To Allan, the world seemed suddenly sick. All the people

in it seemed equally sick. And it was bad enough today. What would it be like tomorrow? he wondered.

Next morning he breakfasted late, waiting for Carson to call him if he was wanted at the office. Both laservid and news-sheet were full of last night's rioting. Not only had the City Council building been attacked but others, taking advantage of the demonstration, had indulged in sheer hooliganism, smashing shop-fronts in the consumer corridors, breaking light globes, and so on. Damage was considerable; arrests had been made, but the Press didn't seem to complain. Instead, they had a better angle to spread:

C.A. MAN GRAPPLES PRESIDENTIAL CANDIDATE!
Alan Powys attacks Fireclown supporters!

A picture showed him wrenching Helen's banner from her grasp. In the story he was described as an angry spokesman for the establishment and Helen as the heroine of the hour, going amongst the people to stand or fall with them. Maybe she had been playing her game better than he had at first thought, he decided.

On the laservid a commentator's voice was heard over the noise of the riot:

"Last night, beautiful would-be President, Miss Helen Curtis, led a peaceful party of demonstrators to the City Council building on Top. They were there to protest against the abuse of Council power which, as everyone knows now, was to take the form of a secret closing of ten of the lowest levels of the City of Switzerland. Miss Curtis and her supporters saw this as a deliberate move to stop free speech, an attempt to silence the very popular figure known as the Fireclown, whose harmless talks have given many people so much comfort and pleasure.

"The peaceful demonstration was savagely broken up by large bodies of policemen who forced themselves through the crowd and began making random arrests almost before the people could lodge their protest.

"It is not surprising that some of the less controlled elements among the demonstrators resisted arrest."

Shot of demonstrator kicking a policeman in the behind.

"Reliable witnesses attest to police brutality towards both men and women.

49

"In the van of the police bully-boys came Alan Powys, grandson of Miss Curtis's rival in the forthcoming Presidential elections—and Assistant Director of City Administration, who had already begun work on closing off the lower levels."

Shot of Alan grappling with Helen.

"But even Mr. Powys couldn't silence the demands of the crowd!"

Shot of him walking away. He hadn't realized laservids were tracking him the whole time.

"And he went back to report his failure to his grandfather, Simon Powys."

Shot of him entering the apartment building.

The cameras panned back to the riot, and the commentary continued in the same vein. He was horrified by the lies—and helpless against them. What could he do? Deny them? Against an already prejudiced public opinion?

"Obviously someone Up There," the commentator was saying, "doesn't like the Fireclown. Perhaps because he's brought a bit of life back into our drab existence.

"This programme decries the totalitarian methods of the City Council and tells these hidden men that it will oppose all their moves to encroach further upon our liberties!"

Fade-out and then fresh shots of a surly-looking man talking to a laservid reporter.

Reporter: "This is Mr. Lajos, who narrowly escaped wrongful arrest in yesterday's demonstration. Mr. Lajos, tell the viewers what happened to you."

Lajos: "I was brutally attacked by two policemen."

Lajos stood staring blankly into the camera and had to be prodded by the reporter.

Reporter: "Did you sustain injuries, Mr. Lajos?"

Lajos: "I sustained minor injuries, and if I had not been saved in time I would have sustained major injuries about my head and body."

Lajos's head seemed singularly free from any obvious injuries.

Reporter: "Did the police give you any reason for their attack?"

Lajos: "No. I was peacefully demonstrating when I was suddenly set upon. I was forced to defend myself . . ."

Reporter: "Of course, of course. Thank you, Mr. Lajos."

Back in the studio, a smiling reporter bent towards the camera.

"It's victory for Miss Curtis and her supporters, folks. The Fireclown won't be bothered by the Council—not so long as we keep vigilant, anyway—for the Council told the people a few minutes ago that . . ."

The picture faded and Carson's face appeared in its place. That was the one irritation of combining communication and entertainment in the single laservid set.

"Sorry if I butted in, Alan. Have you heard the news?"

"Something about me—or about the Council?"

"The Council—they've backed down. They've decided not to close off the levels, after all. Maybe now we can get on with some work. Will you come to the office as soon as you can?"

Alan nodded and put down the news-sheet. "Right away," he said, and switched out.

As he took the fastway to the elevators, he mused over the manner in which the riot had been reported. He was certain that the police had tried not to use violence. Yet, towards the end, they might have lost their patience. These days the police force required superior intelligence and education to get into it, and modern police weren't the good-for-nothing-else characters of earlier times. Still, it could have been that because one side ignored established law and order, so did the other. Violence tended to breed violence.

Violence, he thought, is a self-generating monster. The more you let it take control, the more it grows.

He didn't know it, but he was in for a taste of it.

Two muscular arms suddenly shot out from each side of him. His face slammed against them and he lost his balance on the fastway, falling backwards and sliding along. Two figures rushed along beside him and yanked him onto the slowway.

"Get up," one of them said.

Alan got up slowly, dazed and wary.

He stared at the tall, thin-faced man and his fatter, glowering partner. They were dressed in engineers' smocks.

"What did you do that for?" Alan said.

"You're Alan Powys, aren't you?"

"I am. What do you want?"

"You're the man who attacked Helen Curtis yesterday."

"I did not!"

"You're lying." The man flicked his hand across Alan's face.

51

It stung. "We don't like Council hirelings who attack women!"

"I attacked no one!" Alan prepared, desperately, to defend himself.

The fat man hit him, fairly lightly, in the chest.

On the fastway people were passing, pretending not to notice.

Alan punched the fat man in the face and kicked the thin man's shins.

Neither had expected it. Alan himself was surprised at his own bravery. He had acted instinctively. He was also shocked by his own violence.

Now the pair were pummelling him and he struck back at random. A blow in his stomach winded him, a blow in his face made him dizzy. His own efforts became weaker and he was forced to confine himself to protecting his body as best he could.

Then it was over.

A new voice shouted: "Stop that!"

Breathing heavily, Alan looked up and saw the slightly ashamed face of Tristan B'Ula.

He noticed, too, that all three were wearing a Sun emblem on their clothing—a little metal badge.

The thin-faced man said: "It's Powys—the man who wanted to close the levels. The one who attacked Miss Curtis last night."

"Don't be a fool," B'Ula said angrily. "He didn't want to close the levels; he was taking orders from the Council. I know him—he isn't likely to have attacked Helen Curtis, either."

B'Ula came closer.

"Hello, Tristan," Alan said painfully. "You've started something haven't you?"

"Never mind about that. What *were* you doing last night?" As B'Ula approached, the two men stepped back.

"I was arguing with Helen, telling her she was stupid. Just as you're stupid. None of you know what you're doing!"

"You got a lot of Press cuttings this morning. If I were you I'd stay off the public ways." He turned to the two engineers "Get going. You're nothing better than hoodlums. You pay too much attention to what the Press says."

Alan tried to smile. "The pot calling the kettle black. You

52

started all this, Tris. You should have thought for a while before you began shouting the news about."

"You're damned ungrateful," B'Ula said. "I just saved you from a nasty beating. I did what I had to—I wasn't going to let the Fireclown be shoved around."

"This way, he may get worse," Alan said.

B'Ula grimaced and walked away with the two engineers. Alan looked around for his briefcase but couldn't find it. He got onto the fastway again and took the elevator to the Top, but when he arrived he didn't go to City Administration. He'd heard two people talking in the elevator. There was going to be a debate in the Solar House on last night's riots.

Careless of what Carson would think when he didn't turn up, Alan took a car towards the majestic Solar House where representatives from all over the Solar System had gathered.

He wanted very badly to see his grandfather and his ex-mistress in action.

Solar House was a vast, circular building with tall, slender towers at intervals around its circumference. Each tower was topped by a gleaming glass-alloy dome. The centre of the circle housed the main hall containing many thousands of places for members. Each nation had, like the City of Switzerland, its own councils and sub-councils, sending a certain number of candidates, depending on its size, to the Solar House.

When Alan squeezed his way into the public gallery the House was almost full. Many representatives must have just arrived back in their constituencies after the debate on the outgoing President's policies only to hear the news of the riot, and returned.

Politics hadn't been nearly so interesting for years, Alan thought.

The debate had already opened.

In the centre of the spiral was a small platform upon which sat the President, Benjosef, looking old and sullen; the Chief Mediator, Morgan Tregarith, in ruby-red robes and metallic Mask of Justice; the Cabinet Ministers, including Simon Powys in full purple. In the narrowest ring of benches surrounding the platform were the leaders of the opposition parties—Helen Curtis in a dark yellow robe, belted at the waist, with fluffs of lace at bodice and sleeves; ancient Baron Rolf de Crespigny, leader of the right-wing reactionary Democratic Socialists;

John Holt, thin-lipped in black, leader of the Solar Nationalists; Bela Hakasaki, melancholy-faced Hungarian-Japanese leader of the Divisionists; Luis Jaffe of the New Royalists, and about a dozen more, all representing varying creeds and opinions, all comparatively weak compared with the Solrefs, RLMs, or even the Demosocs.

Behind the circle comprising the opposition leaders all the other Solar representatives sat, first the minor lights in the Solref Cabinet—Denholm Curtis, Under-Secretary for Hydro-Agriculture, was there—then the members of the RLM shadow cabinet; de Crespigny's shadow cabinet shared a tier with John Holt's; behind them were four smaller groups; behind them again six or seven, until, finally, the rank-and-file, split into planets and continents and finally individual nations.

There were probably five thousand men and women in the Solar House, and they all listened carefully as Alfred Gupta, Minister for Police Affairs, answered a charge made by Helen Curtis that the police had used violence towards last night's crowd.

"Miss Curtis has accused Chief of Police Sandai of exercising insufficient control over his officers; that the men were allowed to indulge in offensive language towards members of the public, attacked these members in a brutal manner and did not allow them to lodge a protest which they had prepared for the City Council. These are all grave charges—charges which have also appeared in the Press and on our laservid screens—and Miss Curtis mentions 'proof' of police violence having appeared on those media. If the charges are true, then this is a matter of considerable magnitude. But I suggest that the charges are fabrication, a falsification of what actually happened. I have here a statement from Chief Sandai." He held up a piece of paper and then proceeded to read from it—a straightforward account of what had actually happened, agreeing that some police officers had been forced to defend themselves against the mob, having been pressed beyond reasonable endurance.

Alan had seen one or two of the policemen attack with very little provocation but he felt, from his own observation of the previous night's trouble, that the chief's statement was fairly accurate, although painting his officer's a trifle too white to ring true.

The House itself seemed fairly divided on the question, but

when Helen got up to suggest that the paper contained nothing but lies she was loudly cheered. She went on, in an ironical manner, to accuse the Solar Referendum Government of deliberately provoking the riot by allowing the City Council to close off the levels. Minister for Civil Affairs, Ule Bengtsson, pointed out that it was not the Government's policy to meddle in local politics and that if this matter had been discussed in the Solar House in the first place, then it might have been possible to veto the Council. But no such motion, he observed cynically, had been placed before the House.

This was indisputable.

Alan saw that Helen had decided to change her tactics, asking the President point-blank if it was not the Solar Referendum Party's fixed intention to silence and get rid of the Fireclown who, though he represented no political threat, was in his own way revealing the sterility of the Government's policies in all aspects of life on Earth and beyond it?

Benjosef remained seated. His expression, as it had always been, was strangely affectionate, like an old patriarch who must sometimes chide his children. He spoke from his chair.

"You have heard Miss Curtis accuse my Government of underhand methods in an attempt to rid ourselves of this man who calls himself the Fireclown. I speak in honesty for myself, and for the majority of my Cabinet, when I say we have no interest whatsoever in the Fireclown or his activities so long as they remain within the law. Already"—he glanced at Helen with a half-smile on his face—"it is doubtful whether his supporters have kept within the law, though I have heard that the Fireclown did not encourage last night's riot."

Alan, looking down on the old man, felt glad that someone, at least, seemed to be keeping things in fair perspective.

Then, surprisingly, the House was shaken by a tremendous verbal roar and he saw that several thousand representatives had risen to their feet and were, for the second time in forty-eight hours, shouting the President down.

He saw his grandfather glance towards the Chief Mediator. His features hidden behind his mask, the Mediator nodded. Simon Powys got up and raised his hands, shouting to be heard. Very gradually, the noise died down.

"You do not disbelieve President Benjosef, surely?"

"We do!" Helen Curtis's voice was shrill, and it was echoed by hundreds of others.

"You think the Government is deliberately seeking to outlaw the Fireclown?"

"We do!" Again Helen Curtis's statement was taken up by many of the others.

"And you also think the Fireclown wanted last night's riot?" There was a slight pause before Helen Curtis replied:

"It was the only way his friends could help him. Personally, he is an ingenuous man, unaware of the forces working against him in the Solar House and elsewhere!"

"So you think the rioters were justified?"

"We do!"

"Is this democracy?" Simon Powys said quietly. "Is this what my family and others fought to establish? Is this Law? No—it is anarchy. It is anarchy which the Fireclown has inspired, and you have been caught up in the mood. Why? Because, perhaps, you are too unintelligent, too impatient, to see how mankind may profit from this Law we have created! The Fireclown's babblings are meaningless. He talk of our speech having no meaning and turns sensible individuals into a maddened mob with the choice of a few emotional phrases that say nothing to the mind and everything to the belly! The Fireclown has caught popular fancy. That much is obvious." He sighed and stared around the House.

"I am speaking personally now. For some time I have been aware of the Fireclown's potential ability to whip up the worst elements in human nature. I have seen him as a very great threat to the Solar nation's stability, to our progress, to our development and to individual liberty. And I note from last night's events that I was right . . ."

Alan saw in astonishment that his grandfather's level words had calmed the assembly, that they seemed to be having some effect. He had to admit that the old man seemed to be right, as he'd said. Yet, in a way, his words were *too* convincing. It was still a feeling he had—a feeling that no one in the assembly had as yet discussed anything.

Alan thought that, for them, the Fireclown had ceased to exist. He was witnessing a clash between different ways of thought, not a debate about the Clown at all. He remembered the old Russian technique of choosing a vague name for their enemies and then using it, specifically, to denounce them— attacking the Albanians instead of the Chinese had been one example. Everyone had known who the real enemies were, but there was never a direct reference to them. Still, that had been a calculated technique, rather a good one for its purpose.

But Simon's angry relatives were now using it unconsciously. They were attacking and defending something they were unable to verbalize but which, perhaps wrongly, they were identifying with the Fireclown.

He looked down at the great assembly and for a moment felt pity, then immediately felt abashed by his own arrogance. Perhaps he misjudged them—perhaps they were not less aware but more hypocritical than he thought.

Helen Curtis was speaking again, staring directly into her uncle's eyes as he remained standing up on the platform.

"I have never doubted Minister Powys's sincerity in his denunciation of the Fireclown. But I do say he is a perfect example of the reactionary and conservative elements in the House who are unable to see a *change* as progress. They see their kind of progress, a progress which is inherent in their policies. I see a different kind. Theirs leads to sterility and decay. Ours, on the other hand, leads to an expansion of man's horizons. We wish to progress in many directions, not just one! That is why I see the Fireclown as a victim of the Solref Government. He offers scope and life and passion to human existence. The Solrefs merely offer safety and material comfort!"

"If Miss Curtis had studied the Solar Referendum manifesto in any detail," Simon Powys exclaimed, addressing the assembly, "she would have noted that we are pledged first to forming a strong *basis* upon which future society might work and expand. Evidently, from the mob-worship of this disgusting monster, the Fireclown, we have yet to succeed!"

"You see the Fireclown as a threat! You see him as a monster! You hound this man because, in his naïve and simple manner, he had reawakened mankind's spirit!" Helen spoke directly to Powys, her finger pointing up at him. "Then you are a hollow man with no conception of the realities!"

"So the Fireclown, Miss Curtis tells me, is a happy innocent, bereft of schemes or ambition, a prophet content only to be heard." Powys smiled at the assembly. "I say the Fireclown is a tangible threat and that this madman intends to destroy the world!"

Alan craned forward. His grandfather would not possibly have made so categorical a statement without evidence to back it up.

"Prove it!" Helen Curtis sneered. "You have gone too far in your hatred—senseless and unfounded hatred—of the Fireclown! Prove it!"

Simon Powys's face took on a sterner expression as he turned to speak to the President.

"I have already alerted the City Police," he said calmly, "so there is no immediate danger if they work quickly. There is no question of it—I have been supplied with full proof that the Fireclown is planning to destroy the world by flame. In short, he intends to blow up the planet!"

CHAPTER SIX

ALAN was astounded. For a moment his mood of cynicism held and he was aware of a cool feeling of disbelief as the House, hushed for a second, began to murmur.

Helen suddenly looked frightened. She stared rapidly around the House then up at Powys, whose stern manner could not disguise his triumph.

"Acting on my information, the police have discovered a cache of plutonium war-heads . . ." he continued.

"War-heads!" someone shouted. "We haven't got any! They were outlawed in forty-two!"

"Presumably the Fireclown or some of his friends manufactured them. It is well know that several scientists have been aiding him with his peculiar experiments with fire."

"But he would need fantastic resources!"

Simon Powys spread his hands, aware that his moment of power had come.

"Presumably," he said, "the Fireclown has them. I told you all that he was more than a mere irritation. His power is even more extensive than I at first guessed."

Helen sat down, her face pale. She made no attempt to question Powys's statement. She was baffled, yet as convinced of the truth as everyone else in the House.

The crowd in the public gallery was muttering and shoving to get a closer look at Simon Powys.

The old man's leonine head was raised. Evidently he no longer felt the need for oratory. The House was his.

"If the police discover the war-head cache we shall hear the news in a few moments." He glanced towards the towering central doorway and sat down.

As the tension built up, Alan felt he could take no more of it. He was preparing to turn back into the crowd behind him when a uniformed figure appeared at a side door and made his way down the tiers towards the platform.

It was Chief Sandai, his brown-yellow face shiny with sweat. Watched by everyone, he climbed up the few steps of the platform and approached President Benjosef respectfully.

The microphone picked up his voice and relayed it throughout the House:

"Mr. President, it is my duty to inform you that, acting upon my own initiative, I have declared a state of emergency in the City of Switzerland. A cache of plutonium war-heads equipped with remote control detonators of a type used for setting off bombs from space has been found hidden on the first level. My men have impounded them and await orders."

Benjosef glanced at Powys. "Are you sure you have found all the bombs?" he said.

"No, sir. All we know of are those we found. There could be others. These were stored in a disused war-house cavern."

"You are certain that there was no oversight when the war-house was cleared of its armaments in the past?"

"Perfectly certain, sir. These are new additions. They were being kept in containers previously used for the same purpose, that is all."

Benjosef sighed.

"Well, Minister Powys, this is really your department now, isn't it? How did you find out about the bombs?"

"My secretary, Eugene Junnar, first reported his suspicions to me two days ago. Later investigations proved them to be true. As soon as I knew I informed the police." Powys spoke slowly, savouring his triumph.

Benjosef addressed Chief Sandai. "And have you any evidence to show who was responsible for this illegal stock-pile?"

"Yes, sir. It is almost certain that the man concerned is the individual known as the Fireclown. The chamber was guarded by men known to be in his employ. They at first tried to stop us entering, but offered no physical resistance. One of them has since admitted himself to be a follower of the Fireclown."

"And the Fireclown?" Powys asked urgently.

Chief Sandai swallowed and wiped his forehead. "Not in our custody yet, sir."

Angry impatience passed rapidly across Simon Powys's face before being replaced by a further jutting of the jaw and an expression of resolve. "You had better find him and his accomplices as soon as you can, Sandai. He may well have other bombs already planted. Have you sealed space-ports and checked all means of exit from the City itself?"

"Naturally, sir," Sandai seemed aggrieved.

"Then hurry and find him, man. The existence of the world may depend on locating him and arresting him immediately!"

Sandai galloped down the steps and strode hastily from the House.

Alan didn't wait for any further development in the debate. Simon Powys had made his point, illustrated it perfectly and punched it home relentlessly to the assembly. It was practically certain the Presidency was his.

Pushing through the crowded gallery, he left to take an elevator down and an escalator out of the House. The news must already have leaked to the Press, for laservid reporters were swarming around Chief Sandai, who was obviously flustered and trying to shove his way past them.

Careless of who saw him and the inference that might be put on his act, Alan began to run across the turf towards the nearest elevator cone.

He was sure that his earlier judgment of the Fireclown could not have been so hopelessly wrong. It was only instinct that drove him, but he was so sure that his instinct was right that he was going back, for the second time, to the labyrinthine first level to look at the evidence for himself.

By the time he got to the lower levels another group of vociferous reporters were already on the scene. Police guards surrounded a stack of square, heavy metal boxes, unmarked, at the bottom of the ramp which led down to the first level.

Taking advantage of the police guards' occupation with the reporters, Alan worked his way round them and entered the tunnel which he had gone down earlier—the one which led to the Fireclown's laboratory.

Two guards stood on each side of the entrance. Alan produced his City Administration card and showed it to the men, who inspected it closely.

60

"Just want to look round, sergeant," he said, coolly to one of them. "C.A. would like to know what's going on here so we can take whatever precautions are necessary."

They let him through and he found himself in a big chamber, equipped with all kinds of instruments and devices. He couldn't recognize the purpose of many of them. The place was dark, lit only by an emergency bulb burning near the door. It seemed to have been vacated very rapidly, for there was evidence that an experiment had been taking place and had been hastily abandoned. The door of a cooling chamber was open; broken test tubes crunched beneath his feet; chemicals glinted in the half-light, splashed across floor, benches and equipment. He didn't touch anything but made his way to another door. It was an old fashioned steel door, nearly a foot thick, but it opened when he pushed. In the room the darkness was complete. He went back to find some means of lighting and finally settled for a portable emergency bulb, picking it up by its handle and gingerly advancing into the next room.

The acrid smell of the spilt chemicals was almost unbearable. His eyes watered. This must have been a store-room. Most of the chemical jars were still intact, so were the boxes of spare parts, neatly labelled. Yet there was nothing to suggest any warlike purpose for the laboratory. There was little manufacturing equipment. It was certain the place had only been used for research. Yet, of course, it was possible that a small manufacturing plant might have been housed in another section of the first level.

He came out of the store-room and pushed another door on his left. At first he thought it was locked, but when he pushed again it gave. Whereas the store-room had smelt of chemicals this one smelt merely damp. It was an office. Files and notebooks were stacked around, although a microfile cabinet had been damaged and its contents removed. He noticed also a small, old fashioned, closed circuit television screen and wondered what the cameras were aimed at. He switched it on. The screen flickered and showed part of the corridor outside. He turned the control but each picture showed an uninteresting corridor, a cavern or a room, until he turned once more and the screen brightened to show a well-lighted room.

In it were two men and a woman.

The woman was unknown to Alan. But the men were unmistakable—the skinless Corso, his red, peeled body even more repulsive in good light, and the Fireclown, his great bulk seeming to undulate as he breathed, his face still painted.

Excitedly, Alan tried to get sound, but there appeared to be no sound control on the set. He had no idea where the trio were, but it was fairly certain that cameras were only trained on parts of the first level. Therefore they must be close by.

The woman came up to the Fireclown and pressed her body against him, her right arm spread up across his back, the fingers of the hand caressing him.

He smiled—somehow an extremely generous gesture considering he was now a hunted man—and gently pushed her away, saying something to her. She did not appear annoyed. Corso was more animated. He obviously felt a need for urgency which the Fireclown did not.

Alan suddenly heard a movement in the first chamber and hastily killed the set.

"Mr. Powys, sir?" the sergeant's voice shouted.

"What is it?" he replied, inwardly wishing the man dead.

"Wondered if you were all right, that's the only thing, sir—the smell in here is almost overpowering."

"I'm fine, sergeant, thanks." He heard the sergeant return to his post.

Now he noticed a smaller door leading off the room. It had no lock of any sort, just a projection at the top. He reached up to inspect it when the door wouldn't open. It was a small bar of metal sliding into a socket. He fiddled with it for a while, pulled at it and, at last, the right combination of chances released mechanism and he pulled the door. Alan had never seen a bolt before.

The emergency bulb lit the place and showed him a narrow, low-roofed passage. A rusted sign hung suspended lopsidedly by one chain; the other had broken. Alan caught hold of it, disliking the touch of grimy rust on his fingers, and made out what it said: *Restricted to all personnel!* He let the sign go and it swung noisily against the wall as he continued along the tunnel. Finally he came to another door, but this one would not open at all. He went past it until he reached the end of the tunnel. This was half blocked by the fallen bulk of another massive steel door. He pulled himself over it, wondering if anyone had ever come this way since the lower levels, which had primarily been used for storing armaments, battle-machines and military personnel, had been abandoned with the Great Disarmament of 2042.

A noise ahead of him suddenly startled Alan and he automatically switched off the emergency bulb.

Voices sounded, at first indistinct and then clearer as Alan moved cautiously closer.

"We shouldn't have left those machines intact. If some fool fiddles about with them, heaven knows what'll happen."

"Let them find out." It was the Fireclown's voice, sounding like a pulse-beat.

"And who'll be blamed?" he heard Corso say tiredly. "You will. I wish you'd never talked me into this."

"You agreed with my discoveries, Corso. Have you changed your mind now?"

"I suppose not ... *Damn!*" Alan heard someone stumble. A woman giggled and said: "You're too hasty, Corso. What's the hurry? At present they're combing the corridors they know about. We have plenty of time."

"Unless they find the boat before we get there," Corso said querulously. Alan was creeping behind them now, following them as they moved along in the dark.

"I'm only worried about the fuel. Are you sure we've enough fuel, Corso?" The Fireclown spoke. Although this man had been accused of planning to blow up the world, Alan felt a glow as he listened to the rich, warm voice.

"We wouldn't make Luna, certainly, on what we've got. But we've got enough to take us as far as we want to go."

"Good."

Alan heard a low whine, a hissing noise, a thump, and then the voices were cut off suddenly. A few yards further on his hand touched metal.

He switched on the emergency bulb and discovered that he had come to a solid wall of steel. This was completely smooth and he could not guess how it opened. He tried for almost an hour to get it to work, but finally, his body feeling hollow with frustration, he gave up and began to make his way back in the direction he had come.

A short time later the ground quivered for a few seconds and he had to stop, thinking insanely that the stock-pile of bombs had exploded. When it was over, he thought he could guess what had caused it. The Fireclown had made some reference to a boat—a space-boat. Perhaps that had taken off, though how it was possible so deep underground he couldn't guess.

He was feeling intensely tired. His limbs and his head ached badly and he was incapable either of sustained thought or action. He had to keep stopping every few yards in order to rest, his body trembling with reaction. But reaction to what? To some new nervous or mental shock, or was it the cumulative effect of the past few days? He had been unable to sort out and analyse his emotions earlier, and was even less capable of doing so now.

An acute sense of melancholy possessed him as he stumbled miserably on, at last arriving back at the office. Wearily, he dumped the emergency bulb down in the main chamber, suddenly becoming conscious of a tremendous heat emanating from some source outside. When he reached the entrance the guards had gone. Somewhere in the distance he heard shouts and other noises. As he reached the opening on to the main corridor he saw that it was ablaze with light.

And the light—a weird, green-blue blaze—was coming from the Fireclown's great cavern.

A policeman ran past him and Alan shouted: "What's happening?"

"Fire!" the policeman continued to run.

Now, pouring like a torrent, the flames were eddying down the corridor, a surging, swiftly-moving inferno. There was nothing for the fire to feed on, yet it moved just the same, as if of its own volition.

Fascinated, Alan watched it approach. The heat was soon unbearable and he backed into the chamber.

Only at that moment did it dawn on him that he should have run towards the ramps. He was completely trapped. Also, the laboratory contained inflammable chemicals which would ignite immediately the blaze reached them.

He ran towards the entrance again, stupefied by the heat, and saw that it was too late. The wall of heaving flame had almost reached him.

He still felt no panic. Part of him almost welcomed the flames. But the air was becoming less and less breathable.

He wrenched open doors, looking for another exit. The only possible one seemed to be that which he'd just come back from.

It occurred to him that the Fireclown had been misjudged all round—by everyone except his grandfather who had realized the danger.

The Fireclown had released an inferno on the City of Switzerland. But how? He had never seen or heard of any flames like those which now began to dart around the corridor. He coughed and rubbed the sweat out of his eyes.

At last his brain began to function again. But too late, now, for him to do anything constructive.

Suddenly the entrance was filled with a roaring mass of fire. He retreated from it, hit his back against the corner of a bench, stumbled towards the office. As he slammed the steel door behind him he heard an explosion as the flame touched some of the spilt chemicals.

Air was still flowing in from another source in the small tunnel. He kept the door open.

The other door, sealing off the flames, began to heat and he realized, with fatalistic horror, that when it melted, as it inevitably must, he would die.

He would, he decided, leave the office and head into the tunnel at the last minute. Sitting in the darkness, his confused mind began to clear as the heat rose, and he faced death. A peculiar feeling of calm came upon him and belatedly, he began to think.

The thoughts were not particularly helpful in his present predicament. They told him of no way of escape, but they helped him face the inevitable. He thought he understood, now, the philosophic calm which came to men facing death.

For some days, he realized, he had been moving in a kind of half-dream, grasping out for something that might have been—he hesitated and then let the thought come—love. His emotions had ruled him; he had been their toy, unaware of his motives.

He had always been, to a degree, unstable in this way, perhaps because of his tendency to suppress the unpleasant ideas which sometimes came to him. Having no parents, unloved by his grandfather, his childhood had been spent in a perpetual quest for attention; at school he had been broken of his exhibitionism, and the nature of his job gave him no means of expressing these feelings. Now he sought, perhaps, that needed love in the Fireclown with his constant evoking of parent images. Certainly he had sought it in Helen, so much so that a similar need in her had clashed with his own. And now,

65

spurred on by his grandfather's bitter references to his illegitimacy, he had embarked on a search which had led him to this —death!

He got up, abstractedly watching the door slowly turning red hot.

Had many others, like him, identified the Fireclown with some need to feel wanted?

He smiled. It was too pat, really—too cheap. But he had hit upon a clue to the Fireclown's popularity even if he was not yet near to the exact truth.

Looking at it from another angle, he assembled the facts. They were few and obvious. The Fireclown's own psychological need had created the creed that he had preached, and it had found an echo in the hearts of a large percentage of the world's population. But the creed had not really supplied an answer to their ills, had only enabled them to find expression.

The door turned to smoky white and he smelt the steel smouldering. A slight glow filled the room and his mouth was dry of saliva, his body drained of sweat.

The world had reached some kind of crisis point. Perhaps it was, as the Fireclown had said, because man had removed himself from his roots and lived an increasingly artificial life.

Yet Alan couldn't completely accept this. An observer from another star, for instance, might see the rise and fall of man-made constructions as nothing more than a natural change-process. Did human beings consider an ant-hill 'unnatural'? Wasn't the City of Switzerland itself merely a huge ant-hill?

He saw with surprise that the door had faded from white to red hot and the heat in the room was decreasing. Immediately there was some hope. He forgot his reverie and watched the change intently. Soon the door was only warm to his touch. He pushed at it but it wouldn't budge. Then he realized that the heat had expanded the metal. He waited impatiently, giving an experimental push every now and then until, at last, the door gave and he stepped into the ruined laboratory.

The fire had destroyed much, but now the room swam with liquid. An occasional spurt from the walls close to the ceiling told him the source of his salvation. Evidently the old section of the City had had to protect itself against fire more than any other part—the old automatic extinguishers had finally functioned and engulfed the fire.

In the passage outside it was the same. The extinguishers

had not been tested—not even known about—for years but, activated by the extreme heat, they had finally done the job they had been designed for.

With relief, he began to run up the pitch-dark corridor, at last finding his way to the ramp. A small heap of containers was still there, but there were not so many as he had seen earlier. Had the police managed to take them, or had they been salvaged by the Fireclown? It was, of course, virtually impossible for fire to destroy the P-bombs' shielding, but how many knew that these days? How much panic, Alan wondered, had been the result of the Fireclown's holocaust?

Levels all the way up had been swept by fire. He was forced to push his body on and on, climbing the emergency stairways, avoiding charred corpses and wreckage.

Naked flame had not been used in the city for many years and fire precautions had been lax—there had been no need for them until now.

Alan wondered wryly if the Fireclown's popularity was as great as it had been yesterday.

The first group of men he met were on the fifteenth level. They were forcing open a door in a residential corridor, obviously equipped as a rescue team.

They stared at him, astonished.

"Where did you come from?" one of them asked, rubbing a dirty sleeve over his soot-blackened face.

"I was trapped down below—old fire extinguishers put out the fire."

"They may have put out the fire that the initial fire started," another said, "but they wouldn't have worked on the first lot. We tried. Nothing puts it out once it's under way."

"Then why is it out now?"

"Just thank the stars it is out. We don't know why. It suddenly subsided and disappeared between the fifteenth and sixteenth levels. We can only guess that the stuff it's made of doesn't last forever. We don't know why it burns and we don't know what it burns. To think we trusted the Fireclown and he did this to our homes . . ."

"You're sure it was the Fireclown?"

"Who else? He had the P-bomb cache, didn't he? It stands to reason he had other weapons, too—flame-weapons he'd made himself."

Alan passed on.

The semi-melted corridors gave way to untouched corridors full of disturbed people, milling around men organizing them into rescue teams. Emergency hospital stations had been set up and doctors were treating shock and burn victims, the lucky survivors. The lowest level had been built to withstand destruction of this kind, but the newer levels had not been. If he had been on the tenth-level, or even the ninth where a few families had still lived before the blaze, he wouldn't be alive now.

Though climbing the emergency stairs and ramps was hard going, Alan chose these instead of the overcrowded, fear-filled elevators. On he climbed, grateful for the peace and quiet of the stairs in contrast to the turbulence in the corridors.

He was crossing the corridor of the thirtieth level when he saw that one of the shopfronts—it was a consumer corridor—bore a gaudy slogan. A FREER LIFE WITH THE RLM it said. The place was the election headquarters of the Radical Liberal Movement. Another poster—a tri-di build-up—showed the smiling face of Helen Curtis. At the top, above the picture, it said *Curtis*, and at the bottom, below the picture, it said *President*. The troublesome *for* had been left out.

He stopped and spoke to the door of the place.

"May I come in?"

The door opened. He walked into a poster-lined passage and into a large room stacked with election literature. Bundles of leaflets and posters, all brightly coloured, were stacked everywhere. There didn't seem to be anyone around.

He picked up a plastipaper poster of Helen. An audiostrip in its lining began to whisper softly: *Curtis for President, Curtis for President, Curtis for President*. He flung it down and as it crumpled the whispering stopped.

"I see that's another vote I've lost," said Helen's voice behind him.

"I had a feeling I was going to meet you," he said quietly, still staring at the fallen poster.

"It would be likely, in my own election headquarters. This is only the store-room. Do you want to see the offices? They're smart." Her voice, unlike her words, was not a bit cheerful.

"What are you going to do with all this now?" he said, waving a tired arm around the room.

"Use it, of course. What did you expect?"

"I should have thought a campaign wouldn't have been worth your time now."

68

"You think because I supported the Fireclown when he was popular I won't have a chance now he's unpopular—is that it?"

"Yes." He was surprised. Her spirit, it seemed, was still there. She didn't have a chance of winning the elections now. Was she hiding the fact from herself? he wondered.

"Look, Alan," she said forcefully, "I could have walked into the Presidency without a fight if this hadn't happened. Now it's going to be a tough fight—and I'm rather glad."

"You always liked a fight."

"Certainly—if the opposition's strong enough."

He smiled. "Was that levelled at me by any chance? I've heard it said that if a man doesn't love a woman enough she thinks he's strong; if he loves her too much she thinks he's weak. Was the opposition weak, Helen?"

"You're very sensitive today." Her voice was deliberately cool. "No, I wasn't levelling anything at you. I was talking about your grandfather's happy turn of luck. Our positions are completely reversed now, aren't they?"

"I don't know how I feel about it," he said, stopping the tendency to sulk. Helen's retort had stung him. "I'm not really in support of either of you. I think, on the whole, I favour the RLMs. They could still win the constituency elections, couldn't they, even if you didn't get the Presidency? That would give you a strong voice in the House."

"If they kept me as leader, Alan." Her face softened as she admitted a truth which previously she had been hiding from. "Not everyone who approved of my stand yesterday approves of it today."

"I hate to say I warned you of it. You should have known better, Helen, than to go around whipping up mobs. People have to trust politicians as well as like them. They want a modern, up-to-date President, certainly—but they also want a respectable one. When the voters sit down and think about it, even if this Fireclown business hadn't taken the turn it has, they'll choose the candidate they can feel confidence in. Fiery politics of your sort only work for short spells, Helen. Even I know that much. Admittedly, after showing yourself as a 'Woman of the People' you could have stuck to parliamentary debate to make your points and probably danced home. But now you've identified yourself so strongly with the Fireclown that you haven't a hope of winning. I should give it up." He looked at her wistfully.

She laughed shortly, striding up and down between the bales of posters. "I haven't a dog's chance—you're right. But I'll keep on fighting. Lucky old Simon, eh? He's now the man who warned the people of their danger. Who else could they vote for?"

"Don't get bitter, Helen. Why don't you start painting again? You know what you're doing in that field. Really, even I know more about politics than you do. You should never have entered them. There are people who are natural born politicians, but you're just not one of them. I've asked you this a dozen times previously, but I'd still like to know what makes you go on with it."

"One of the strongest reasons is because the more people disapprove of my actions, the harder I pursue them. Fair enough?" She turned, staring at him quizzically with her head cocked on one side.

He smiled. "In a word, you're just plain obstinate. Maybe if I'd encouraged you in your political work you might have been a well-known painter by now—and well rid of all this trouble."

"Maybe. But it's more than that, Alan." She spoke softly, levering herself up on to one of the bales. She sat there swinging her legs, looking very beautiful. She no longer wore the make-up she'd had on earlier. "But I've got myself into this now, and I'm going to stick at it until the end. Sink or swim."

He told her about his visit to the first level—omitting that he'd heard the Fireclown and his friends leaving—and of his narrow escape.

"I thought I was going to be killed," he said, "and I thought of you. I wondered, in fact, if we weren't both searching for the same thing."

"Searching? I didn't know you were the searching kind, Alan."

"Until this Fireclown business blew up, I was the hiding kind. I hid a lot from myself. But something grandfather said must have triggered something else in me." He paused. "Was it only three days ago?" he mused wonderingly.

"What did he say?"

"Oh," Alan answered lightly, "he made a rather pointed reference to the fact that my ancestry isn't all it might be."

"That was cruel of him."

"Maybe it did me good. Maybe it brought something into the open. Anyway, I started getting curious about the Fireclown. Then you visited me and I was even more curious. Perhaps because you associated yourself with the Fireclown's creed, I associated him with you and it led on from there. I went to see the Fireclown the same night, you know."

"Did you speak to him personally?" She sounded envious.

"No. I never got to see him, actually. But I attended yesterday's 'audience'. I thought I understood why you supported him. In his own heavy way he made sense of a kind." He frowned. "But the same could be said for grandfather, I suppose. That was a good speech this morning."

"Yes, it was." She was staring at him, her mouth slightly open, her breasts moving beneath her lacy bodice more rapidly than usual.

"I'm glad all this has happened," he continued. "It's done a lot of good for me, I think."

"You're glad about the P-bombs being found—about the fire, too?"

"No. I couldn't really believe the Fireclown was guilty until I saw the evidence for myself. And I still don't hate him for what he tried to do—for what he still might try to do, for that matter. I feel sorry for him. In his own way he *is* the naïve and generous giant you tried to tell me about."

"That's what I think. You were down there—were you satisfied that the Fireclown was responsible for stockpiling those bombs and starting the fire?"

"The evidence was plain, I'm afraid."

"It's idiotic," she said angrily. "Why should he do a thing like that? A man so full of *love!*"

"Love—or hate, Helen?"

"What do you mean?"

"He professed to love mankind—but he hated mankind's works. He hated what he thought were our faults. Not exactly true love, eh?"

"We'll never know. I wonder if he escaped. I hope he has—so long as he doesn't try any more sabotage."

For the second time in the last few days Alan found himself concealing something from his ex-mistress. He didn't tell her that he knew the Fireclown had managed a getaway, at least from Earth. Instead, he said: "Should he escape? After all, he was responsible for the deaths of least a hundred people. The residential corridors on nine and ten all the way up to fifteen were full of corpses. Probably a great many more were roasted

71

in their homes. A nasty death, Helen. I know. I came close to it myself. Should he escape without punishment?"

"A man like the Fireclown is probably not conscious of his crime, Alan. So who's to say?"

"He's intelligent. I don't think he's insane, in any way we can understand. *Warped*, perhaps. . . . ?"

"Oh, well, let's stop talking about the Fireclown. There's a world-wide search out for him now. The fact that he vanished seems to prove his guilt, at least for Simon Powys and the public. I've noticed a few remained loyal to the Fireclown for some time after they found out about the bombs. If the fire hadn't started he'd probably still have strong support from people who thought the bombs were planted."

"You can't plant a stack of P-bombs, Helen. The Fireclown must have made them. He's the only one with the resources."

"That's what everyone thinks. But a few of us politicians know better, Alan."

"Nuclear weapons have been banned for years. What are you talking about?"

"Not everyone gave up all their stock-pile in the early days of the Great Disarmament, Alan. There were quite a few who hung on to some secret arms piles until they saw how things were going. Of course, when the Solar Government was found to work and the threat of war dwindled away to nothing, they forgot about them or got rid of them."

"Good God! Nuclear bombs. I'm not superstitious. War's a thing of the past. But it seems dreadful that the weapons should still be around."

"There are plenty," she said ironically. "At least enough to fight a major solar war!"

CHAPTER SEVEN

ALAN, like the rest of his contemporaries, had lived so long in a peaceful world that the concept of war, particularly war fought on a nuclear scale, was horrifying. For nearly a century the world had hovered on the brink of atomic conflict, but time after time governments had just managed to avoid it. With the final outlawing of nuclear weapons in 2042, a great sigh of relief had gone up. The human race had come dangerously close to destroying itself, but at last it could progress without that fear forever pressing on it.

And now Helen's casual reference to a solar war!

"You don't mean that as a serious suggestion, did you?" he asked her.

"Alan, the Solar Cabinet, myself and one or two other party leaders have been aware of the existence of nuclear arms for some time. Simon Powys, in his speech before the House this morning, could not reveal that, because if the news leaked we might well have a fresh panic on our hands. Anyway, it suited his purpose to suggest that the Fireclown manufactured them. The Fireclown might have been able to make his, but he could just as easily have bought them."

"Bought—?" Alan gasped. "Bought them from whom?"

"From one of the men who specialize in such things. Over the years there has been a constant 'black market' in nuclear arms. The police have been aware of it and they have been vigilant. Many of those who discovered forgotten caches have been arrested and the weapons destroyed. But some haven't. And these men would welcome physical conflict— preferably on Earth or between Earth and *one* of the other worlds, so that they could get to safety on the unthreatened world. If one side began an attack with nuclear arms, the other would have to defend itself—and the dealers could then get any price that they wanted."

"But, surely, arms dealing on such a scale is impossible!"

"Not if the cards are played right. And it has been evident to me for some time that someone *is* playing their cards right. If he gets the hand he wants—bang! Suddenly, overnight, without any kind of warning and none of the psychological protection people perhaps had a hundred years ago, we'd be plunged into a war of colossal destruction."

"I can't believe it!"

"Perhaps it's better. Remember, this is only what the dealers wish for—it might not happen. That's why it's so secret. It might be possible to remove the danger once and for all with none of the public knowing it was there. The RLM shadow cabinet have a plan to prevent the eventuality; Simon Powys has another. I think ours is better. Now you know one of the reasons I'm in politics and why I stay in."

"I'll accept that," he said a trifle dubiously. "Do you think the Fireclown's tied up with any of these dealers?"

"If he's tied up with one, he's probably tied up with them all. Those we haven't caught are the most powerful and have very likely formed themselves into a syndicate. That's what the rumours say, at any rate."

"I saw no evidence of a plant when I explored the Fireclown's level. So it's probable that he could have bought the P-bombs."

"There's another angle to it," Helen said thoughtfully. "Admittedly I may not have been wholly objective about the Fireclown, but what if the dealers had *planted* the P-bombs on him, knowing that someone would eventually find out?"

"Why should they do that?" Alan bent down and picked up a handbill, his eyes fixed on it. It was another picture of Helen, this time in an heroic pose. Fifty words of text underneath briefly outlined her ideals in purple adjectives.

"The arms dealers want a war—preferably one that wouldn't have too destructive results and wouldn't involve all three habitable planets. First, hint that the Fireclown has a stock-pile, supply the evidence to be found, take advantage of the scare—and the possibility of the Fireclown possessing more weapons—then unload a ready-made batch of weapons for 'defence' or the Solar Government. That way, you see, there might not be a war at all—but the dealers would profit just the same."

"That sounds close to the truth—if the dealers did frame the Fireclown, of course. But we have proof that he caused the destruction of fifteen levels. How do you explain that? That fire was impossible to extinguish. He had obviously made it, in the same way he manufactured that weird artificial sun in the cavern."

"He may have been pushed into it—self-defence."

"No, I don't think so."

"There's one way we can get more information," she said briskly, jumping down off the bale. "We can go and see Simon Powys. He'd know more about it than anyone."

"Do you want to do that?"

"I'm curious. More than that, Alan." She smiled nervously. "I may be able to wheedle something out of the old patriarch that would be advantageous to me in the election. If I could prove that Fireclown was framed it would help a lot."

He shook his head, wondering at her incredible optimism. "All right," he said. "Let's go."

Simon Powys received them with the air of the conquering Roman general receiving the defeated barbarian leaders. All he needed, Alan thought, was a toga and a laurel crown.

He smiled urbanely, greeted them conventionally, offered them drinks, which they accepted.

"Come into the study," he said to his grandson and niece. He led the way. He had furnished the place with deliberate archaism. There were even a few family portraits—of the best-remembered members of the Powys clan. The first Denholm, Alan and Simon Powys hung there, as well as the two women Presidents of the Solar Government. A proud and slightly sombre-looking group. The bookcases were of mahogany, filled primarily with books on politics, history and philosophy. The novels were of the same type—political novels by Disraeli, Trollope, Koestler, Endelmans and De la Vega. Alan rather envied his grandfather's one-track mind. It made him good at his career.

"To tell you the truth," Simon Powys said heavily. "I feel sorry for you both. You were misled, as most people were, and this business must have left you slightly in the air. It hasn't done you much good politically, has it, Helen? A pity—you've got good Powys stuff in you—strong will, impersonal ambition . . ."

"And an eye to the main chance." She smiled. "Though you'll probably say, uncle Simon, that I lack self-discipline and could do with a spot more common-sense. You'd probably be right about the self-discipline. I lost out on that one—I think I'm finished now, don't you?"

Alan admired her guile.

Simon Powys nodded regretfully. He probably did regret his niece's political demise, just as he obviously regretted Alan's never having shown an interest in politics. "Still, you were rather foolish, y'know."

"I know," she said contritely.

He turned to Alan. "And you, my boy? I suppose you understand why I was so adamant earlier?"

"Yes, grandfather."

The old man seemed to warm to both of them. "I shall be
75

President, no doubt, when the next session begins. It was really my last opportunity to take such high responsibility—family tradition demands a Powys of every generation to serve at least one term. I was hoping that you, Alan, would follow on, but I suppose the task will fall to Helen's son and Denholm's. I wish my daughter . . ." He cleared his throat, seemingly moved to strong emotion, although Alan thought the last line had been a bit stagey. It was probably for his benefit. He wondered why he should have felt such momentary love for his grandfather at their earliest interview.

"What made you suspicious of the Fireclown in the first place?" Helen said, in the manner of a whodunit character preparing the detective for his denouement.

"Instinct, I suppose. Could have told you there was something fishy about him the first time I heard of him. Made Junnar go down and have a look the first opportunity he could. There was also another business which I can't really talk about . . ."

"He knows about the illegal stock-piles, uncle," Helen said forthrightly.

"Really? A bit unwise to spread it around, isn't it?"

"I'm not in the habit of betraying confidences, grandfather," Alan said tritely, with a hard look at Helen.

"No. I suppose it's all right. But presumably Helen has impressed you with the need for secrecy?"

"Of course," Helen said.

"Well, I had a feeling he'd been connected with the dealers. They're the only group of criminals powerful enough to hide a man and help him change his identity. I guessed that he had probably come from their hideout, though this was all conjecture, you understand. The police investigated him and could find nothing to indicate it, though they agreed with me."

"So, in fact, unless it can be established that the P-bombs are part of the old stock, there is nothing to connect him with the dealers?" Helen said, trying hard not to show her disappointment.

"I have already been in touch with the laboratory analysing the bombs. They tell me they *are* old stock—you would have discovered that soon, anyway, at the next Committee meeting. Obviously we can't tell the public that."

"Obviously," said Helen, "though it might have strengthened my own case in the House slightly."

76

"Not to any important degree."

"What's this committee?" Alan asked curiously.

"We call it the One Hundred Committee, after a slightly less effective British anti-nuclear group which existed in the middle of the twentieth-century. Actually there are only ten of us. The Committee is pledged to locating every single nuclear weapon left over from the old days and seeing the offenders punished where possible. We work, of course, in close collaboration with the highly secret ARP—the Arms Removal Police. Our work has been going on for years. Helen is the secretary and I am the chairman. Other important politicians comprise the remaining eight."

"Very worthy," said Alan. "Are you effective?"

"We have been in the past, though our job is becoming more difficult since the dealers work together, pooling their resources. They would welcome an opportunity to sell what they have —perhaps Helen has already told you."

"Yes, she has. But it occurred to me that you could offer to buy the dealers out now. Surely it would be better to pay their price and have the arms without waiting for a crisis to decide you?"

"That's our main bone of contention," Helen put in. "Uncle doesn't agree wth buying them now. I want to do that."

"The fantastic price these brigands would demand would beggar the Solar nation," Simon Powys said gruffly to his grandson. "We must do it in secret and justify the expenditure at the same time. It would be impossible. I feel they'll overstep the mark at some stage, then we'll catch them."

"The expenditure's worth it!" Helen said. "We could recuperate from poverty, but survival in a nuclear war . . . !"

"If we caught the Fireclown, then," Alan said slowly, "it might give us a lead to the arms dealer."

"Possibly," Powys agreed, "though he might not admit to it. Secondly, he might not even know who the dealers are. They are naturally extremely cautious. However, they are certainly going to take advantage of the trouble the Fireclown has caused. The man must be caught—and destroyed before he makes any more trouble!"

"Grandfather!" Alan was shocked. The death penalty had been abolished for more than a hundred years.

"I'm sorry—I'm extremely sorry, Helen. You must forgive

77

an old man's tongue. These concepts were not quite so disgusting when I was a young man. Certainly we must imprison or exile the Fireclown."

Alan nodded.

"It's funny he said, "that the Fireclown should preach a return to nature; that, in fact, science leads to mankind's destruction, and yet he should be planning that same destruction—or at very least is a tool of those who would welcome it."

"Life," said the old man with the air of a philosopher, "is full of that sort of paradox."

CHAPTER EIGHT

"I'LL see you home," Alan said lightly as they left the apartment.

"That would be nice," she said.

They walked slowly through the gardens, repaired and beautiful again. The starlight was augmented by soft beams from the roof structure which had the appearance of many tiny moons shining down, each one casting a single, exquisite beam. The Top had been well designed. To live here was the ambition of every young man and woman. It gave people, thought those at the Top, something to aim for.

"If only I could speak to the Fireclown personally," Helen said wistfully. "Then at least I'd be able to form a better idea of what he's really like."

Alan preferred to say nothing.

They reached the door of her apartment on the sixty-third level and went in. Familiar smells greeted him, smells which he always associated with Helen—fresh, slightly scented, of soap and oils. It was strange, he reflected, that women's apartments always seemed to smell better than men's. Maybe it was an obvious thought. He noticed he was breathing a little more quickly, slightly more shallowly.

Neither recognized by outward expression the thought that was in their minds, yet each was aware of the other's emotions. Alan was slightly fearful, for he remembered the conflict between them as well as their old happiness and realized that Helen probably did, too.

"Would you like a nightcap?" she invited.

"I'd prefer coffee, if you've got it." Unconsciously, he had given her her opportunity. He was torn now, half afraid of what seemed likely to happen.

She came over to him as he sat down in a comfortable chair beside a small shelf of book-tapes.

She leaned down and stroked his face lightly.

"You look dreadfully tired, Alan."

"I've had a hard day." He smiled. He took her hand and kissed it.

"I'll go and get the coffee," she said.

When she came back she had changed into a pair of chaste pyjamas and a robe of thick, dark blue material. She had a tray of coffee—real coffee from the smell. She put it down on a table and drew up a chair so that the table was between them.

Helen, he thought, *Oh, Helen, I love you.* They were staring at each other, both wondering, perhaps, if this reunion would take on the same pattern as their previous affair.

"We're wiser now," she said softly, handing him his coffee. "It's a Powys trait—we learn by our mistakes."

"There are always different mistakes to be made," he warned her. It was the last attempt to retreat from the situation and allow her to do the same, as gracefully as possible.

"That's experience," she said, and the fears were forgotten. Now they looked at one another as if they were new friends.

When they made love that night it was entirely different from anything either had ever before experienced. They treated one another delicately, yet passionately, as if a return to their earlier, less self-conscious love would plunge them back into the turmoil of four months before.

In the morning Alan's arm was aching painfully from having cradled her head all night. He raised her head gently and propped himself on his elbow, tracing the softness of her shoulder with his fingers. She opened her eyes and seemed to be looking at him like a respectful stranger. Presumably there was a similar expression in his own face, for he felt he shared her emotion. He kissed her lightly on the lips and pushed back the bed clothes, swinging himself out of the narrow bed.

He sat slightly hunched on the edge, studying his head and torso reflected in the mirror opposite.

"I've got an idea where the Fireclown is," he said suddenly. She was half asleep and didn't seem to hear him.

79

He didn't repeat himself then but went into the kitchen to make coffee. He was feeling rather tired now and his legs shook a little as the machine came alive and produced two beakers of hot coffee. He transferred the coffee into cups and took them back.

She was sitting up.

"What did you say about the Fireclown? You know where he is?"

"No, but we might be able to guess." He told her about overhearing the trio in the passage.

"Why didn't you tell me about this yesterday?"

"That was yesterday," he said simply. She understood and nodded.

"They took off in a small space-boat. I've thought about it since and I think there must be a launching ramp leading through the rock to somewhere outside the City. Those old bombs had to be launched from somewhere."

"That sounds logical. You say he remarked that they didn't have enough fuel to make Luna. They may have made a transcontinental flight."

"Unlikely. You can't land even a small rocket without at least a few people observing it. I've got a feeling they're orbiting—maybe waiting for someone to pick them up."

"Or they may have gone to St. Rene's?"

"Why should they do that?" The Monastery of St. Rene Lafayette was the home of a group of monks who practised a form of scientific mysticism. Little was known about the Order and it was thought that the monks were harmless. The monastery was, in fact, an abandoned space-station which the monks had taken over. The world had decided they were quaintly mad and had all but forgotten them.

"Well," Helen said, sipping her coffee, "it's just a connection that my mind made. I associated one 'crank' with a group of others, I suppose."

"Unless they *were* orbiting, it's the only place they could have gone," Alan agreed. "I wonder how we could find out."

"By going there, perhaps."

"We'd need a boat. We haven't got one."

"My brother has. A nice job—one of the latest Paolos."

"Would he let us take it?"

"We don't need to ask. I often use it. I have a pilot's licence,

80

the audiolocks respond to my voice, the ground staff at the port know me—we'd have a good chance of getting away with it."

"And going to our deaths, maybe. The Fireclown appears to be more ruthless than we thought, remember?"

"But are the monks? They are bound to give sanctuary to those they term 'unclears', I believe."

"It's worth a try." He got up. "I'm going to have a bath. Is my green suit still here?"

"Yes."

"Good." He glanced at the chronom on the wall. "It's still early. If we leave now we could . . ." He turned to her. "Where is your brother's ship?"

"Hamburg—she's a sea-lander."

"A fast cab could get us there in an hour. You'd better get up and get ready." He grinned at her as she sprang out of bed.

Hamburg Spaceport was surrounded by a pleasant garden-city with a population of less than two millions. In contrast to the capital city of Switzerland, its buildings were single- or double-storied. Beyond the spaceport buildings water glinted in the summer sun, beneath a pale and cloudless blue sky. As the cab spiralled down towards the landing roof a huge bulbous ship suddenly erupted from the waves, water boiling to steam as it lumbered upwards.

Helen pointed: "The *Titan*, bound for Mars and Ganymede, probably carrying one of the last seed consignments they need."

By the time the cab brought them down on the roof the ship had disappeared. From his lodge, the only building on the roof, an official in a brown velvet cutaway and baggy, cerise pantaloons came sauntering towards them. He was a firm-faced man with a smile.

"Good morning, Miss Curtis. Sorry to hear about yesterday," he said. "Many people's faith in the Fireclown seems to have been misplaced."

"Yes, indeed," said Helen, forcing a smile in response to his. "I'm planning to make a pleasure trip until the fuss dies down. Is the *Solar Bird* ready?"

"I expect so. She was being checked in the locks, I believe. She should be okay now. Do you want to go straight down?"

"Yes, please."

He took them into his lodge, a neat office with a big window overlooking the sea which was still heaving and steaming after the *Titan*'s take-off. A small elevator cage was set in one wall. The man opened the gate for them, glancing at Alan in a speculative way. Alan returned his stare blandly and followed Helen into the elevator. It began to hiss downward.

A man in coveralls let them out, a plum, red-faced man with a mechanics badge on his sleeve.

"Good morning, Miss Helen. Nice to see you."

"Good morning, Freddie. This is Mr. Powys—Freddie Weinschenk."

They shook hands and Weinschenk led them along an artificially lit corridor. Alan had never been in Hamburg before, but he knew the general design of a modern spaceport. They were now below ground level, he guessed, heading along a tunnel which led under the sea-bed.

Finally, Freddie ordered a door to open and they were in a dark, cool chamber with metal walls. From one wall, the back half of a small space-yaught projected, seeming, at first, to be stuck on the wall until Alan realized that the other half lay outside and that they were actually in a pressure chamber.

"Thanks, Freddie." Helen went up to the airlock and spoke to it. It began to slide open; then slowly the four doors all opened and they went into the cramped cabin of the ship. Freddie shouted from outside:

"If you're leaving immediately, miss, I'll start the chamber up."

"Thanks, Freddie. See you when we get back."

Helen went to the control panel and touched a stud. The airlocks closed behind them. She switched on the exterior viewer so they could see the chamber. Freddie had left and Alan saw that the room was swiftly being flooded. Soon it was full and the wall surrounding the ship began to expand away from the ship itself and he saw the ramp extending outwards into open sea.

"We'll make a soft take-off," Helen said, strapping herself in the pilot's couch. Alan got into the other couch. "We don't want anyone to think we're in a hurry," she added.

"The softer the better," he smiled. "I've only been into space once and I didn't much care for the trip. She was an old chemical ship and I was certain she was going to break down every inch of the journey."

"You'll see a lot of difference in the *Solar Bird*." She activated the drive. "It's unlikely they could improve a nuclear ship any further. They'll have to start thinking of some new type of engine now, I suppose, just as the old type starts getting familiar and comfortable."

The control panel was alive now, its instruments measuring and informing.

Alan felt a double pounding beat for a second or so, and then the ship was speeding up the ramp, leaving it, plunging up through water and then was in daylight, racing into the sky.

She switched on the chart-viewer, selected the area of space she wanted. It showed her the position of the space-station monastery and gave her all the information she needed.

"I hope your hunch is right," she said and turned round to see that Alan had blacked out.

There had been no reason for this at all, since the mounting pressure outside was completely countered by the ship's internal mechanisms. It was probably some kind of reflex, she decided.

"I'm a fool," he said when he was awake again. "*Did* anything happen, or was it just my imagination."

"Just imagination, I'm afraid. But you needed the sleep, anyway."

"Where are we?"

"In orbit. We should be getting pretty close to the station in a little while. For the time being I'm going to pretend we're in trouble—that way we'll lull any suspicions the monks might have if they *are* harbouring the Fireclown."

Soon the wheel of the big station came in sight, the sun bright on its metal. There were two ships they could see hugged in its receiving bays, a big one and a little one. The big one was of unfamiliar design. They could see its title etched on its hull from where they were. *Pi-meson*.

"Funny name for a ship," Alan commented.

"The monks—if it *is* their ship—have got funny ideas." She reached out to press a red stud. "That's the May-day signal. With any luck they should get it."

In a moment their screen flickered and a face appeared on it—a thin man, lean-nosed and thin-lipped.

"Would it be impertinent to deduce that you are in trouble?" he said.

"It wouldn't be, no," Helen replied. "Can you help us?"

"Who knows? Can you manoeuvre your ship so that we can grapple, or shall we send out help?"

"The steering seems to be all right," she said. "I'll come in."

She coasted the ship until they were near one of the empty bays and the station's magnegraps pulled them into the bay.

When, finally, they climbed from their ship into the unpleasant air of the monastery, they were greeted by the thinfaced monk. He was dressed in a blue habit that did nothing for his already pale face. His hair was short but he had no tonsure. His eyes and cheeks were sunken but, in his own way, he looked healthy enough. He held out a skeletal hand with incredibly long fingers.

"I am Auditor Kurt," he said as Alan shook hands. "It is good that we can be of service to you. Please come this way."

He took them into a small, barely furnished room and offered them tea, which they accepted.

"What exactly is wrong with your ship?" he asked politely.

"I'm not sure. I'm not familiar with the type—it's new. I could not get the landing jets to work when I tested them preparatory to re-entering the atmosphere. It's just as well I did test them." She had personally jammed the jet control. It could be fixed easily.

"You were lucky to be so close." The monk nodded.

Alan was wondering how he could find out if Fireclown was here.

"I'm extremely interested in your Order," he said conversationally. "I'm something of a student of religions—perhaps you can tell me about yours?"

"Only that we were founded as long ago as 1950, although this Order did not come into existence until 1976 and did not come here until about twenty years ago. We are a branch of the original faith, which did not pay a great deal of attention to its mystical aspects until we founded the Order of St. Rene. St. Rene is not the true name of our inspired founder—that is secret to almost all—but that is the name we use for him."

"I should like to see the monastery. Is that possible?" Alan looked around the small room, avoiding the monk's intent gaze.

"Normally it would be possible—but, ah, we have repairs

going on in many parts . . . We are not really prepared for visitors."

"Oh? Then whose is the ship, other than ours, in the receiving bay?"

"Which one?"

"There are two. The *Pi-meson* and the *Od-Methuselah*."

"Both ours," the monk said hastily. "Both ours."

"Then why did you ask which one I spoke of?"

The monk smiled. "We monks have devious minds, I'm afraid. It is the nature of our calling. Excuse me, I'll go and check that the mechanics are repairing your ship." He rose and left. They heard the door seal itself behind him. They were locked in.

Alan sipped his tea.

"If the Fireclown's here, they're not likely to let on to outsiders who'd take the news back to Earth," he said.

"We'll have to think of a means of getting a look around this place. Have you noticed the atmosphere? It's weird."

The atmosphere of the place fitted well with the space-station monastery circling in space, away from the things of Earth. It had a detached air of calm about it, and yet there was a feeling of excitement here, too. It was possible, of course, that he was imagining it, for he was very excited himself.

"Do you think they know what he's up to? Or is he just making use of their habit of affording people sanctuary?" Alan asked her.

"They seem unworldly, to say the least," she replied, shivering a little, for the room was not well heated.

The door opened and Auditor Kurt came back.

Your boat has been fixed, my friends. I see from the registration plates that it is owned by Denholm Curtis—an important man on Earth, is he not?"

"He's my brother," Helen said, wondering if the monk was getting at anything in particular.

Alan became aware at last that they might be in danger. If the Fireclown was here and knew they were here, too, he might decide it was risky to let them go.

"So you are Helen Curtis. Who, then, is this gentleman?"

"I'm Alan Powys."

"Ah, yes, Simon Powys's grandson. From what I have seen of recent lasercasts, Miss Curtis and Minister Powys are at odds over certain issues. Which side do you support, Mr. Powys?"

"Neither," Alan said coldly. "Just call me a disinterested spectator.

A peculiar expression came on the monk's face for a second. Alan could work out what it indicated.

"I should say you were the least disinterested . . ." the monk mused. Then he said briskly: "You asked earlier if you could look over the monastery. To tell you the truth we are not always willing to let strangers inspect our home, but I think it would be all right if you wanted to take a quick tour before you leave."

Why the monk's sudden change? Was he planning to lead them into some sort of trap? Alan had to take the chance.

"Thanks a lot," he said.

They began to walk along the curving corridor. This part, the monk told them, was reserved for the monks' cells. They turned into a narrower corridor which led them to another similar to the one they'd just left, though the curve was tighter.

"Here is what we term our clearing house." The monk smiled, opening a door and letting them precede him through. It was a fairly large room. Several monks sat on simple chairs. They were dressed in brown dungarees. The monk in the centre was dressed, like Auditor Kurt, in a blue habit, and was chanting some sort of litany.

"How would you worry somebody?" he chanted.

"By destroying their confidence," the other monks mumbled in reply.

"How would you make somebody happy?"

"By casting forth their engrams," said the monks in unison.

"How would you help somebody?"

"Teach them to be clear."

"By the Spirit of the Eight Dynamics," intoned the blue-clad monk, "I command thee to cast forth thy engrams forth-with!"

The monks seemed to freeze, concentrating intently. Above them, behind the monk in the blue habit, a weird machine whirred and buzzed, dials swinging around strangely marked faces, lights flashing.

Alan said respectfully: "What are they doing?"

"They are attempting to learn the ultimate secret of the Great Triangle," Auditor Kurt whispered.

"Ah," Alan nodded intelligently.

They left this room and entered another. Here a great screen was blank and there were comfortable chairs scattered around before it.

"Sit down," said Kurt. "We are expecting a special event, today."

Alan and Helen sat down and watched the screen.

They fidgeted for over half-an-hour as nothing happened, and Kurt continued to watch the screen impassively, not looking at them.

Alan's sense of danger was heightened and he had a feeling the monk was deliberately keeping them in suspense.

Then, all at once, big letters began to form on the screen until a whole sentence was emblazoned there.

ANOTHER BROTHER CLEAR! said the message. It meant nothing to either of them.

Alan turned to the monk, half suspicious that a trick had been played on them, but the monk was looking ecstatic and incredibly pleased.

"What does it *mean*?" Alan asked desperately.

"What it says—the hampering engrams have been exorcised from one of our brothers. He is now a clear and ready to become a Brother Auditor, as I am. It is a time for rejoicing in the monastery when this comes about."

Alan scratched his head and looked at Helen, who was equally perplexed.

"Well," beamed thin-faced Auditor Kurt, "now you have seen a little of our monastery."

Half convinced that he was the victim of a practical joke, Alan nodded mutely. He was no nearer to finding out if the Fireclown was here, although perhaps a check on the *Pi-meson* when they got back to Earth would help them.

"Thank you for showing us," Helen said brightly. She, too, was obviously uncertain of what to do next.

"Oh"—the monk seemed to remember something—"there is one other thing I should like to show you before you leave. Will you follow me?"

They walked until they were close to the centre of the space-wheel, came to a small door in the curved wall of Central Control. Auditor Kurt ordered it open. It hissed back and they stepped through.

"Good afternoon, Mr. Powys," said the Fireclown amiably.

CHAPTER NINE

"SO you *did* come here," Helen blurted out.

"I have no idea how you deduced it." He grinned. "But I must praise your intelligence. I hope no one else on Earth thinks as you do."

Alan kept silent. They would be safer if they didn't tell the Fireclown how they had worked out his hiding place. He looked around. Corso and the woman were also there, lounging in their seats and staring amusedly at the rest.

He felt dwarfed by the Fireclown's bulk, not only physically —the man stood at least six foot six—but also psychologically. He could only stare stupidly, unable to say anything. Yet it was peculiar. Now that they were face to face he did not feel afraid any longer. The man's strange magnetism was tangible, and once again he found himself liking the Fireclown, unable to believe that he had committed an act of mass murder and plotted to blow up the Earth.

"So you are Alan Powys," mused the Fireclown, as if the name had some special meaning. His face was still heavily painted, with wide lips and exaggerated eyes, but Alan could make out the features under the paint a little clearer. They seemed thoughtful.

"And why are you here, anyway?" Corso said, moving his repulsive red and glinting body in the chair.

"To ask questions," Helen said. She was pale and Alan could understand why—the skinless man took a lot of getting used to.

"Questions!" The clown's body moved in a great shrug. He turned his back on them and paced towards his seated friends. "Questions! By the solar firmament! What questions can I answer?"

"They are simple—and demand only simple replies, if you are truthful with us."

The Fireclown whirled round and laughed richly. "I never lie. Didn't you know that? I never lie!"

"But perhaps you mislead," Alan said quietly. "May I sit down?"

"Of course."

They both sat down.

"We want to know if you planned to blow up the world," Helen said with a trace of nervousness in her voice.

"Why should I? I wanted to save it, not hurt it."

"You did a good job with the fire which swept Switzerland," Alan retorted.

"Am I to blame for that? I warned them not to tamper."

"Are you trying to tell us you weren't responsible for that fire?" Alan said grimly.

"I've been watching the lasercasts. I'm aware of what's being said of me now. They are fickle, those people. If they had really listened to me this would not have happened. But nobody listened properly."

"I agree with that." Alan nodded. "I saw them—they were using you as a means of rousing their own latent emotions. But you should have known what you were doing and stopped!"

"I never know what I am doing. I am . . ." The Fireclown paused and glared at him. "I was *not* responsible for the fire. Not directly, at any rate. Some of those policemen must have tampered with my fire machines. They are very delicate. I have been experimenting with means of controlling chemical and atomic fire. I produced that little artificial sun and could have produced more if I had not been interrupted by those meddlers."

"Why are you experimenting with fire? What's your purpose?" Helen leaned forward in her chair.

"Why? I have no reasons. I am the Fireclown. I have no purpose save to exist as the Fireclown. You do me too much honour, Miss Curtis, to expect action and plans from me. For a time I spoke to the people in Switzerland. Now that's over I shall do something else." He roared with laughter again, his grotesque body shaking.

"If you have no plans, no thought for the future, then why did you buy P-bombs from the arms dealers?"

"I know nothing of bombs or dealers! I had no inkling that those bombs were in my cavern!"

Either he was blinded by the Fireclown's overpowering presence or the man was telling the truth, Alan felt. He seemed to have a lusty disregard for all the things that concerned Helen and himself. He did not seem to exist in the time and space that Alan shared with the rest of the human race, seemed

89

to tower over it, observing it with complete and amused detachment. But how far could he trust this impression? Alan wondered. Perhaps the Fireclown was the best actor in the world.

"You must know something of what's happening!" Helen exclaimed. "Your appearance at a time of acute crisis in society's development could not be mere coincidence."

"Society has had crisis before, young lady." Again he shrugged. "It will have others. Crises are good for it!"

"I thought you ingenuous, then I changed my mind. I can't make you out at all." She sank back into the chair.

"Why should you make me out? Why should you waste time trying to analyse others when you have never bothered to look within yourself? My own argument against machines and machine-living is that it hampers man from really looking into his own being. You have to take him away from it, put him in the wilderness for a short time, before you can see that I speak truth. In my way I worship the sun, as you know. Because the sun is the most tangible of nature's workings!"

"I thought you represented a new breakthrough in thought," Helen said quietly. "I thought you knew where you were going. That is why I supported you, identified myself and my party with you."

"There is no need to seek salvation in others, young lady!" Again he became disconcertingly convulsed with that weird and enigmatic laughter.

She got up, bridling.

"Very well, I've learnt my lesson. I believe you when you say you weren't planning destruction. I'm going back to Earth to tell them that!"

"I'm afraid Mr. Corso here, who advises me on such matters, has suggested that you stay for a while, until I am ready to leave."

Alan saw his logic. "When are you leaving?" he said.

"A few days, I expect. Perhaps less."

"You won't, of course, tell us where." Alan smiled at the Fireclown for the first time and when the man returned his smile, grotesquely exaggerated by the paint around his lips, he felt dazzled, almost petrified with warmth and happiness. It was the Fireclown's only answer.

Why did the Fireclown have this ability to attract and hold people just as if they were moths drawn to a flame?

Auditor Kurt had left the room while they were conversing. Now he returned with another man behind him.

"A visitor for you, Fireclown."

Both Alan and Helen turned their heads to look at the newcomer. He was a small, dark man with a moody face. A marijuana was between his lips.

"I commend you on your choice of rendezvous," he said somewhat mockingly. His hooded eyes glanced at the others in the room, stopped for a moment on Alan and Helen. He looked questioningly at the Fireclown. "I hope you haven't been indiscreet, my friend."

"No," said the Fireclown shortly. He chuckled. "Well, Mister Blas, have you brought what I wanted?"

"Certainly. It is outside in the ship I came with. We must talk. Where?"

"Is this not private enough for you?" the Fireclown asked petulantly.

"No, it is not. I have to be over-cautious, you understand."

The Fireclown lumbered towards the door, ducking beneath it as he made his way out. "Corso," he shouted from the corridor, "you'd better come, too."

The skinless man got up and followed Blas from the room. The door closed.

"Blas," Helen said forlornly. "So the Fireclown has been lying to us."

"Who is he?"

"Suspected head of the arms syndicate." She sighed. "*Damn*! Oh, damn the Fireclown!"

The woman, a full-bodied brunette with a sensuously generous mouth, got up from her seat.

She stared down at Alan, regarding him closely. Helen glared at her.

"And what part do you play in this?" she asked.

"A very ordinary one," she said. "The Fireclown's my lover."

"Then your lover's a cunning liar," Helen snorted.

"I shouldn't condemn him until you know what he's doing," the woman said sharply.

The three of them were alone together now that Kurt had left too.

"You're disappointed, aren't you?" the woman said, looking candidly at Helen. "You wanted the Fireclown to be some sort of saviour, pointing the direction for the world to go. Well, you're wrong. And those who think he's a destroyer are wrong also. He is simply what he is—the Fireclown. He acts according to some inner drive which I have never been able to fathom and which I don't think he understands or bothers about himself."

"How long have you known him?" Helen asked.

"Some years. We met on Mars. My name's Cornelia Fisher."

"I've heard of you." Helen stared at the woman in curiosity. "You were a famous beauty when I was quite young. You disappeared suddenly. So you went to Mars. Hardly the place for a woman like you, was it? You must be over forty but you don't look thirty."

Cornelia Fisher smiled. "Thanks to the Fireclown, I suppose. Yes, I went to Mars. The life of a well-known 'beauty', as you call me, is rather boring. I wasn't satisfied with it. I wasn't satisfied with anything. I decided that I was leading a shallow existence and thought I'd find a deeper one on Mars. Of course I was wrong. It was merely less comfortable"—she paused, seeming to think back—"though the peace and quiet helped, and the scenery. I don't know if you've seen it since the revitalization plan was completed, but it is very beautiful now. But I never really lost my ennui until I met the Fireclown."

"He was a Martian, then?" Alan knew there were a few families of second and third generation colonists responsible for working on the revitalization project.

"No. He came to Mars after a space-ship accident. He's from Earth originally. But I don't know much more about him than you do. Once you've been with the Fireclown for a short time, you learn that it doesn't matter who he is or what he does—he's just the Fireclown, and that's enough. It's enough for him, I think, too, though there are strange currents running beneath that greasepaint. Whether he's in control of them or not, I couldn't say."

"His connection with Blas seems to disprove part of what you've said." Alan spoke levelly, unable to decide what to think now.

"I honestly don't know what he and Blas are doing." Cornelia Fisher folded her arms and walked towards her handbag which lay on the chair she'd vacated. She opened it and took out a packet of cigarettes. Alan tried to look unconcerned but he had never seen a nicotine addict before. She offered them defiantly. They both refused, with rapid shakes of their heads. She lit one and inhaled the smoke greedily. "I'd swear he's not buying arms. Why should he? He has no plans of the kind Earth condemns him for having."

"Maybe he doesn't tell you everything," Helen suggested.

"Maybe he doesn't tell me anything because he hasn't got anything to tell me. I don't know."

Alan went to the door and tested it. It was shut firmly.

"Judging by the evidence," he said, "I can only suppose that the accusations made by my grandfather against the Fireclown are basically correct. Those P-bombs were part of the arms syndicate's stock—and we have seen that the Fireclown already knows Blas, who you say, Helen, is the head of the syndicate."

"It's never been proved, of course," she said. "But I'm pretty sure I'm right."

"Then the world *is* in danger. I wonder if the Fireclown would listen to reason."

"His kind of reason is different from ours," said Cornelia Fisher.

"If I see him again, I'll try. He's too good to get mixed up in this sordid business. He has a tremendous personality—he could use his talents to . . ." Alan's voice trailed off. What could the Fireclown use his talents for?

Cornelia Fisher raised her eyebrows. "His talents to do what? What does safe little Terra want with men of talent and vision? Society doesn't need them any more."

"That's a foolish thing to say." Helen was angry. "A complex society like ours needs expert government and leaders more than ever before. We emerged from muddle and disorder over a hundred years ago. We're progressing in a definite direction now. We know what we want to do, and if Blas and his friends don't spoil it with their plots and schemings we'll do it eventually. The only argument today is *how*. Planned progress. It was a dream for ages and now it's a reality. Until this arms trouble blew up there were no random factors. We had turned politics into an exact science, at long last."

"Random factors have a habit of emerging sooner or later," Alan pointed out. "If it wasn't the nuclear stock-piles it would have been something else. And those random factors, if they don't throw us too far out of gear, are what we need to stop us getting complacent and sterile."

"I'd rather not be blown to smithereens," Helen said.

"The Fireclown isn't a danger to you, I know." Cornelia Fisher sounded as if she was less convinced than earlier.

"We'll soon know if the ARP fail to get hold of those stockpiles." Helen's voice sounded a bit shaky. Alan went over to her and put his arm round her comfortingly.

A short time later the Fireclown returned, seemingly excited. Blas was not with him. Alan couldn't guess at Corso's expression. He could only see the red flesh of his face, looking like so much animated butcher's meat.

"Did you get some more P-bombs?" Helen asked mockingly. The Fireclown ignored her.

Corso said: "What are you hinting at, Miss Curtis?"

"I know Blas is head of the arms syndicate."

"Well, that's more than we do. Blas is supplying us with materials for our ship, the *Pi-meson*, which we badly need. There has been no talk of armaments."

"Not a very convincing lie," Helen sneered.

Now Corso also ignored Helen. He watched the Fireclown in a way that a mother cat might watch her young—warily yet tenderly. Corso seemed to play nursemaid to the clown in some ways.

"It will take time to fit," said the Fireclown suddenly. "But thank God we could get them. We couldn't possibly have made them ourselves."

His gaudy red and yellow costume swirled around him as he turned to grin at Alan.

"I wonder if you'd want to," he mused mysteriously.

"Want to what?" Alan asked.

"Come for a trip in the *Pi-meson*. I think it would do you good."

"Why me? And what kind of good?"

"You could only judge that for yourself."

"Then you could dispose of us in deep space, is that it?" Helen said. "We've seen too much, eh?"

The Fireclown heaved a gusty sigh. "Do as you like, young woman. I've no axe to grind. Whatever takes place on Earth has no importance for me now. I tried to tell the people something, but it's obvious I didn't get through to them. Let the darkness sweep down and engulf your hollow kind. I care not."

"It's no good." Helen shook her head. "I can't believe anything you say. Not now."

"If you had it wouldn't have made any difference." Corso's

ghastly face grinned. "The rest of the world lost faith in their idol, and the world hates nothing so much as an idol who turns out to have feet of clay! Not, of course, that the clown wished to be one in the first place."

"Then why did you start that set-up on the first level? Why did he make speeches to thousands? Why did he let them adore him at his 'audiences'?" Helen's voice was high, near-hysterical.

As Alan watched and listened, a mood of absolute detachment filled him. He didn't really care about the pros and cons any more. He only wondered what the Fireclown's reasons were for suggesting the trip.

"The Fireclown was originally living down there in secret. We were working on our machines. We needed help—scientists and technicians—so we asked for it, got it. But the scientists told their friends about the Fireclown. They began to ask him about things. He told them. All he did, in the final analysis, was supply an outlet for their emotional demands."

Helen fell silent.

Alan came to a decision.

"I'd like to take that trip," he said—"if Helen can come, too."

"Good!" The Fireclown's resonant voice seemed suddenly gay. "I should like to take you. I'm glad. Yes, Glad."

Both Alan and Helen waited for the Fireclown to add to this statement, but they were disappointed. He went and leaned against a bulkhead, his great face bent towards his chest, his whole manner abstracted.

Was he thinking of the trip? Alan wondered. Or had he simply forgotten about them now they had agreed to go?

Somehow, he felt the latter was the more likely answer.

The Fireclown seemed a peculiar mixture of idiot and intellectual. Alan decided that he was probably insane, but what this insanity might lead to—the destruction of Earth?—could not easily be assessed. He must wait. And perhaps he would learn from the trip, wherever it took them. Mars, possibly, or Ganymede.

CHAPTER TEN

HELEN was getting understandably restless. Five hours had passed and the Fireclown still stood in the position he had taken up against the bulkhead. Corso and Cornelia Fisher had talked sporadically with Alan, but Helen had refused to join in. Alan felt for her. She had placed all her hopes on gaining information from the Fireclown and, he guessed, she had desperately wanted him to disprove the allegations now being made against him on Earth. But, frustratingly, they were no nearer to getting an explanation; were worse confused, if anything.

If he had been studying any other individual, Alan would have suspected the Fireclown of sleeping with his eyes open. But there was no suggestion of slumber about the clown's attitude. He was, it seemed, meditating on some problem that concerned him. Possibly the nature of the problem was such that an ordinary man would see no logic or point in solving it.

The Fireclown seemed to exist in his own time-sphere, and his mind was unfathomable.

At last the grotesque giant moved.

"Now," he rumbled, "the *Pi-meson* will be ready. We have been lucky to find shelter with the monks, for they are probably the only men who can come close to understanding the nature of the ship, and doubtless they will have done their work by now. Come." He moved towards the door.

Alan glanced at Helen and then at the other two. Corso and Cornelia Fisher remained where they were. Helen got up slowly. The Fireclown was already thumping up the corridor before they reached the door.

"I hope you know what you're doing," she whispered. "I'm afraid, Alan. What if his plan *is* to kill us?"

"Maybe it is." He tried to sound self-possessed. "But he could do that just as easily here as in deep space, couldn't he?"

"There are several ways of dying." She held his hand and he noticed she was shivering. He had never realized before that anyone could be so afraid of death. Momentarily he felt a sympathy with her fears.

They followed the gaudy figure of the Fireclown until they reached the bay section.

Auditor Kurt was there.

"They have just finished," he told the Fireclown, spinning the wheel of the manually operated airlock. "Your equations were perfectly correct—it was we who were at fault. The field is functioning with one hundred per cent accuracy. Five of us were completely exhausted feeding it. Blas being able to supply those parts was a great stroke of luck."

The Fireclown nodded his thanks and all three stepped through the short tunnel of the airlocks and entered a surprisingly large landing deck. Alan, who had seen the *Pi-meson* from space, wondered how it could be so big, for a considerable portion of spaceships was taken up with engines and fuel.

Touching a stud, the Fireclown closed the ship's lock. A section of the interior wall slid upwards, revealing a short flight of steps. They climbed the steps and were on a big control deck. The covered ports were extremely large, comprising more than half the area of the walls. Controls varied—some familiar, some not. And there were many scarcely functional features—rich, red plush couches and chairs, fittings of gold or brass, heavy velvet curtains of yellow and dark blue hung against the ports. It all looked bizarre and faintly archaic, reminding Alan, in a way, of his grandfather's study.

"I shall darken the room," the Fireclown announced. "I can operate the ship better that way. Sit where you will."

The Fireclown did not sit down as Alan and Helen sat together in one of the comfortable couches. He stood at the controls, his huge bulk blotting out half the instruments from Alan's sight. He stretched a hand towards a switch and flicked it up. The lights dimmed slowly and then they were in cold blackness.

Helen gripped Alan's arm and he patted her knee, his mind on other things as a low whining arose from the floor.

Alan sensed tension in the Fireclown's movements heard from the darkness. He tried to analyse them but failed. He saw a screen suddenly light with bright whiteness, colour flashed and swirled and they saw a vision of space.

But against the darkness of the cosmos, the spheres which rolled on the screen, flashing by like shoals of multi-coloured billiard balls, were unrecognizable as any heavenly bodies Alan had ever seen. Not asteroids by any means, not planets—they were too solid in colour and general appearance; they shone, but not with the glitter or reflected sunlight. And they passed swiftly by in hordes.

Moved by the beauty, astonished by the unexpected sight, Alan couldn't voice the questions which flooded into his mind.

In the faint light from the screen the Fireclown's silhouette could be seen in constant motion. The whining had ceased. The spheres on the screen began to jump and progress more slowly. The picture jerked and one sphere, smoky blue in colour, began to grow until the whole screen itself glowed blue. Then it seemed to burst and they flashed towards the fragments, then through them, and saw—a star.

"Sol," commented the Fireclown.

They were getting closer and closer to the sun.

"We'll burn up!" Alan cried fearfully.

"No—the *Pi-meson* is a special ship. I've avoided any chance of us burning. See—the flames!"

The flames . . . Alan thought that the word scarcely described the curling, writhing wonder of those shooting sheets of fire. The control deck was not noticeably warmer, yet Alan felt hot just looking.

The Fireclown was roaring his enigmatic laughter, his arm pointing at the screen.

"There," he shouted, his voice too loud in the confines of the cabin. "There, get used to that for a moment. Look!"

They could not help but look. Both were fascinated, held by the sight. And yet Alan felt his eyes ache and was certain he would be blinded by the brightness.

The Fireclown strode to another panel and turned a knob.

The port coverings began to rise slowly and light flowed in a searing stream into the cabin, brightening everything to an extraordinary degree.

When the ports were fully open, Alan shouted his wonder. It seemed they were in the very heart of the sun. Why weren't they made sightless by the glare? Why didn't they burn?

"This is impossible!" Alan whispered. "We should have been destroyed in a second. What is this—an illusion of some sort? Have you hypno—?"

"Be quiet," said the Fireclown, his shape a blob of blackness in the incredible light. "I'll explain later—if it is possible to make you understand."

Hushed, they let themselves be drawn out into the dancing glare.

Alan's soul seemed full for the first time, it even seemed natural that he should be here. He felt affinity with the flames. He began to identify with them, until he *was* them.

Time stopped.

Thought stopped.

Life alone remained.

Then blackness swam back. From far away he observed that his rigid body was being shaken, that a voice was bellowing in his ear.

". . . you have seen! You have *seen!* Now you know. *Now* you know! Come back—there is more to see!"

Shocked, it seemed, back into his body, he opened his eyes. He could see nothing still, but felt the grip on his shoulders and knew that the Fireclown, his voice excited—perhaps insane —shouting from in front of his face. "That is why I call my- self the Fireclown. I am full of the joy of the flames of life!"

"How . . . ?" The word stumbled hoarsely from his lips.

But the Fireclown's hands left his shoulders and he heard the man screaming at Helen, shaking her also.

There could be no fear now, Alan decided. Though, earlier, he might have been perturbed by the Fireclown's ravings, he now half ignored them, aware that there was no need to listen.

What he demanded now was an explanation.

"How could we have seen that and lived?" he shouted roughly, groping out to seize the Fireclown's tattered clothing and tug at it. "How?"

He heard Helen mumble. Satisfied, the Fireclown moved away from her, jerking himself free from Alan's grip.

He got up and followed the Fireclown through the black- ness, touched his body again, sensing the tremendous strength in the man.

The Fireclown shook with humour again.

"Give me a moment," he laughed. "I have to feed the ship further directions."

Alan heard him reach the control panel, heard him make adjustments to studs and levers, heard the now familiar whine. He groped his way back to Helen. She put her arms round him. She was crying.

"What's the matter?"

"Nothing. Really—nothing. It's just the—the emotion, I suppose."

The lights came on.

Arms akimbo, the Fireclown stood grinning down at them.

"I see you are somewhat stunned. I had hoped to turn you mad—but you are obviously too entrenched in your own narrow 'sanity' to be helped. That grieves me."

"You promised me you would explain," Alan reminded him shakily.

"If you could understand, I said, if you remember. I'll explain a little. I am not yet ready to tell you my full reason for bringing you with me. Now, see . . ." He turned and depressed a stud and a section of one port slid up to reveal normal space, with the sun flaring—still near, but not so near as to be dangerous. "We have returned to our ordinary state for a while. Now you see the sun as any traveller would see it from this region of space. "What do you think of it?"

"Think of it? I don't understand you."

"Good."

"What are you getting at?"

"How important do the conflicts now taking place on Earth seem to you now?"

"I haven't . . ." He couldn't find the words. They *were* important, still. Did the Fireclown think that this experience, transcendental as it might have been, could alter his view of Earth's peril?

Impatiently, the Fireclown turned to Helen.

"Is your ambition to become president of Earth still as strong as it was, Miss Curtis?"

She nodded. "This—vision or whatever it was—has no bearing on what are, as far as you're concerned, mundane problems relating to our society. I still want to do my best in politics. It has changed nothing. I have probably benefited from the experience. If that's the case, I shall be better equipped to deal with Earth affairs."

The Fireclown snorted, but Alan felt Helen had never sounded so self-confident as she did now.

"I still want to know how you achieved the effect," Alan insisted.

"Very well. Put simply, we shunted part of ourselves and part of the ship out of normal time and hovered, as it were, on its edges, unaffected by many of its rules."

100

"But that's impossible. Scientists have never . . ."

"If it was impossible, Alan Powys, it couldn't have happened and you couldn't have experienced it. As for your scientists, they have never bothered to enquire. I discovered the means of doing this after an experience which almost killed me and certainly affected my thought-processes.

"The sun almost killed me, realize that. But I bear it no malice. You and I and the ship existed in a kind of time freeze. The ship's computer has a 'mind' constructed according to my own definitions—they are meaningless to the rigidly thinking scientists of Earth but they work for me because I am the Fireclown!

"I am unique, for I survived death by fire. And fire gave my brain life—brought alive inspiration, knowledge!" He pointed back at the sun, now dwindling behind them.

"There is the fire that gave birth to Earth and fed its denizens with vitality. Worship it—worship it in gratitude, for without it you would not and could not exist. *There* is truth—perhaps the sum of truth. It flames, living, and *is*; self-sufficient, careless of *why*, for *why* is a question that need not—cannot—be answered. We are fools to ask it."

"Would you, then, deny Man his intellect?" Alan asked firmly. "For that is what your logic suggests. Should we have stayed in the caves, not using the brains which"—he shrugged—"the sun, if you like, gave us? Not using an entire part of ourselves—the part which sets us over the animals, which enabled us to live as weaklings in a world of the strong and the savage, to speculate, to build and to plan? You say we should be content merely to exist—I say we should think. And if our existence is meaningless then our thoughts might, in time, give it meaning."

The Fireclown shook his painted head.

"I knew you would not understand," he said sadly.

"There is no communication between us," Alan said. "I am sane, you are mad."

The Fireclown, for the first time, seemed hurt by Alan's pronouncement. Quietly, without his usual zest, he said: "I know the truth. I know it."

"Men down the ages have known a truth such as the one you know. You are not unique. Fireclown. Not in history."

"I am unique, Alan Powys, for one reason if none other. I have seen the truth for myself. And you shall see it, perhaps. Did you not become absorbed into the fire of the sun? Did you not lose all niggling need for meaning therein?"

"Yes. The forces are overwhelming, I admit. But they are not everything."

The Fireclown opened his mouth and once more bellowed with laughter. "Then you shall see more."

He closed the port and the room darkened.

"Where are we going?" Helen demanded grimly, antagonistically.

But the Fireclown only laughed, and laughed, and laughed, until the strange spheres began to roll across the screen again. Then he was silent.

CHAPTER ELEVEN

HOURS seemed to pass and Helen dozed in Alan's arms. Alan, too, was half asleep, mesmerized by the coloured spheres on the screen.

He came fully awake as the spheres began to jerk and slow. A bright red filled the screen, divided itself into fragments.

More spheres appeared, but these were suns.

Suns. A profusion of suns as closely packed as the planets to Sol. Huge, blue suns, green, yellow and silver suns.

A thousand suns moving in stately procession around the ship.

The screens slid up from the ports and light, ever changing, flickered through the cabin.

"Where are we?" Helen gasped.

"The centre of the galaxy," the Fireclown announced grandly.

All around them the huge discs of flame, of all colours and all possible blends of colour, spun at extraordinary speeds, passing by in an orbit about an invisible point.

Alan, once again, could not retain his self-possession. Something within him forced hm to look and wonder at the incredible beauty. These were the oldest suns in the galaxy. They had lived and died and lived again for billions of years. Here was the source of life, the beginnings of everything.

Though the Fireclown would probably have denied it, the vision was—profound. It had significance of such magnitude that Alan was unable to grasp it. Philosophically, he resigned himself to never knowing what the experience implied. He felt that the Fireclown's belief of existence without significance beyond itself was preposterous, yet he could see how one could arrive at such a conclusion. He himself was forced to cling to his shredding personality. The whirling stars dwarfed him, dwarfed his ideas, dwarfed the aspirations of humanity.

"Now," chuckled the Fireclown in his joyous insanity, "what is Earth and all its works compared with the blazing simplicity of—*this!*"

Helen spoke with difficulty. "They are—different," she said. "They are linked, because they all exist together, but they are different. This is the order of created matter. We seek an order of cognizant matter and the stars, however mighty, however beautiful, have no cognizance. They might perish at some stage. Man, because he thinks, may one day make himself immortal —not personally, perhaps, but through the continuance of his race. I think that is the difference."

The Fireclown shrugged.

"You have wondered what is real, have you not? You have wondered that we have lost touch with the realities, we human beings; that our language is decadent and that it has produced a double-thinking mentality which no longer allows us contact with the natural facts?"

He waved his hands to take in the circling suns.

"Intelligence! It is nothing, it is unimportant, a freak thrown up by a chance combination of components. Why is intelligence so esteemed? There is no need for it. It cannot change the structure of the universe—it can only meddle and spoil it. *Awareness*—now, that's different. Nature is aware of itself, but that is all—it is content. Are we content? No! When I go to Earth and try to convey what I know to the people, I am conscious of entering a dream world. They cannot understand me because they are unaware! All I do, sadly, is awaken archetypal responses in them which throws them further out, so they run around like randy pigs, destroying. Destroying, building, both acts are equally unimportant. We are at the centre of the galaxy. Here things exist. They are beautiful but their beauty has no purpose. It is *beauty*—it is enough. They are full of natural force but the force has no expression; it is force alone, and that is all it needs to be.

"Why ascribe meaning to all this? The further away from

the fundamentals of life we go, the more we quest for their meaning. There *is* no meaning. It is here. It has always been here in some state. It will always be here. That is all we can ever truly know. It is all we should want to know."

Alan shook his head, speaking vaguely at first. "A short time ago," he said, "I was struck by the pettiness of political disputes, horrified by the ends to which people would go to get power—or 'responsibility' as they call it—feeling that the politicians in the Solar House were expending breath on meaningless words . . ."

"So they were!" the Fireclown bellowed back at him approvingly.

"No." Alan plugged on, certain he was near the truth. "If you wished to convince me of this when you took us on this voyage, you have achieved the opposite. Admittedly, as one observes them at the time, the politicians seem to be getting nowhere, society detaches itself further and further from the kind of life its ancestors lived. Yet, seeing these suns, entering the heart of our own sun, has shown me that this stumbling progress—unaware gropings in the dark immensity of the universe, if you like—is as much a natural function as any other."

Gustily, the Fireclown sighed.

"I felt I could help you, Alan Powys. I see you have fled further back into your fortress of prejudice." He closed the port covers. "Sit down—sleep if you wish. I am returning to the monastery."

They berthed and entered the monastery in silence. The Fireclown seemed depressed, even worried. Had he seen that, for all his discoveries, for all his vision and vitality, he was not necessarily right? Alan wondered. There was no knowing. The Fireclown remained still the enigmatic, intellectual madman— the naïve, ingenuous, endearing figure he had been when Alan first saw him.

Auditor Kurt greeted them. "We are looking at our weekly lasercast. Would you like to come and watch? It might interest you."

He took them to a small room where several monks were already seated. Corso was there, too, and Cornelia Fisher. At the door the Fireclown seemed to rouse himself from his mood.

"I have things to consider," he told them, walking away down the corridor.

They went in and sat down. The laserscreen was blank.

Evidently the amount of laser-viewing allowed the monks was limited.

Corso came and sat next to them. Alan was getting used to his apparently skinless face.

"Well," he said good-naturedly, "did your voyage enlighten you?"

"In a way," Alan admitted.

"But not in the way he intended, I think." Helen smiled a trifle wistfully, as if she wished the Fireclown had convinced them.

"How did he hit on the discovery that enables him to travel so easily and to such dangerous parts?" Alan said.

"Call it inspiration," Corso answered. "I'm not up to understanding him, either, you know. We were co-pilots on an experimental ship years ago. Something went wrong with the ship —the steering devices locked and pushed us towards the sun. We managed, narrowly, to avoid plunging into the sun's heart and went into orbit. But we were fried. Refrigeration collapsed slowly. I suffered worse in some ways. It took my skin off, as you can see. My fellow pilot—the Fireclown to you, these days —didn't suffer so badly physically, but something happened to his mind. You'd say he was mad. I'd say he was sane in a different way from you and me. Whatever happened, he worked out the principle for the *Pi-meson* in the Martian hospital— we were rescued, quite by chance, by a very brave crew of a freighter which had gone slightly off course itself. If that hadn't happened, we'd both be dead now. We were in hospital for years. The clown pretended amnesia and I did the same. For some reason we were never contacted by Spaceflight Research."

"How did you get the money to build the *Pi-meson?*"

"We got it from Blas, the man you accused of being an arms dealer. He thinks the ship is a super-fast vessel but otherwise ordinary enough. He supplied us with computer parts this time."

"Where is Blas now?"

"The last I heard he had a suite at the London Dorchester."

"The Dorchester? That's reasonable—a man could hide in the Mayfair slums and nobody would know."

"I think you don't do Blas justice. He's an idealist. He wants progress more than anyone. He wouldn't have any part in blowing the world up. At least . . ." Corso paused. "He's a funny character, but I don't think so."

Alan was quiet for a while. Then he said:

"After that trip, I think I do believe you when you say you're not implicated in the arms dealers' plans—not knowingly, anyway. At least the Fireclown has satisfied me on that score, even if he didn't achieve his main object." He turned to Helen. "What about you?"

"I agree." She nodded. "But I'd give a lot to know Blas's motives in helping you." She looked at Corso. "Are you telling us everything?"

"Everything I can," he said ambiguously.

The laserscreen came to life. A news broadcast.

The newscaster bent eagerly towards the camera.

"It's fairly sure who the next President will be, folks. Simon Powys, the one man to recognize the peril that the world is in from the infamous Fireclown's insane plot to destroy the world, is top of this station's public opinion poll. His niece, the only strong opponent in the elections which begin next week, has dropped right down. Her violent support of the Fireclown hasn't helped a bit. Rumour circulates that Miss Curtis and Minister Powys's grandson, Alan Powys, have disappeared together. Strange that two people who were seen publicly fighting in the recent riots should have teamed up."

Shot of Simon Powys in his home, a smug expression on his powerful old face.

Reporter: "Minister Powys, you were the first to discover the bomb plot. How did it happen?"

Powys: "I suspected the Fireclown from the start. I don't blame people for being duped by his talk—we're all human, after all—but a responsible politician has to look below the surface . . ."

Reporter (murmuring): "And we're all very grateful."

"I made sure that a constant check was kept on his activities," Simon Powys continued, "and thus was able to avert what might have been a terrible crime—the ultimate crime, one might say. Even now the threat of this man still trying to bombard the Earth from some secret hiding place is enormous. We must be wary. We must take steps to ensure his capture or, failing that, ensure our own defence."

"Quite so. Thank you, Minister Powys."

"Everything's calm again in Swiss City," announced the

newscaster as he faded in, "and we're back to normal after the riots and subsequent fire which swept sixteen levels yesterday. The Fireclown's victims number over three hundred men, women—and little children. We were all duped, folks, as Minister Powys has pointed out. But we'll know better next time, won't we? The freak hysteria has died as swiftly as it blew up. But now we're watching the skies—for the search for the Fireclown seems to prove that he has left Earth and may now be hiding out on Mars or Ganymede. If he's got bombs up there, too, we must be ready for him!"

Although angered, Alan was also amused by the lasercaster's double-thinking ability. He, like the rest, had done a quick about-face and now Simon Powys, ex-villain and victimizer, was the hero of the hour.

But the hysteria, he realized, had not, in fact, died down. It had taken a different turn. Now there was a bomb scare. Though he hadn't planned it that way, Alan thought, Simon Powys could easily be falling into the arms syndicate's plot, for this scare was just what they needed to start trouble. As soon as he got the chance he was going to tell the police about Blas and the Dorchester—or else go there himself and confront the arms dealer.

He didn't bother to watch the lasercast but turned to Helen.

"We'd better try to get the Fireclown to let us go as soon as possible," he said worriedly. "There's things to be done on Earth."

"Apart from anything else," she pointed out, "I've got an election to fight!"

A chuckle behind her, full-throated and full of humour, made her turn and look up at the Fireclown's gaudy bulk filling the doorway.

"You are persistent, Miss Curtis. Even a journey into the heart of the sun does nothing to change your mind. You'll be pleased to hear that we are leaving very soon and you'll be able to return to Earth. But first . . ." He looked directly at Alan, stared into his eyes so that Alan felt a strange thrill run through him, partly fear, partly joy. There was no doubt that the Fireclown's magnetism was something apart from his strange ideas. "I must talk with you, Alan Powys—alone. Will you follow me?"

Alan followed. They entered a room decorated with marvel-
107

lous oil paintings, all of them depicting the sun seen in different ways.

"Did you do these?" Alan was impressed as the Fireclown nodded. "You could have put more across to the public by displaying them than with all that talking you did," he said.

"I didn't think of it. These are private." The Fireclown indicated a metal bench for Alan to sit on. "No one comes here but me. You are the first."

"I feel honoured," Alan said ironically. "But why me?"

The Fireclown's huge chest heaved as he took an enormous breath. "Because you and I have something in common," he said.

Alan smiled, but kindly. "I should say that's extremely unlikely judging by our earlier conversations."

"I don't mean ideas." The Fireclown moved about—like a caged lion. There was no other analogy to describe his restless pacing, Alan thought. "I regret that I've been unable to convince you. I regret it deeply, for I am not normally given to regretting anything, you know. What happens, happens—that is all. I should have said we have *someone* in common."

"Who?" Alan was half dazed already, for he thought he knew what the Fireclown was going to say.

"Your mother," grunted the Fireclown. The words took time coming out of this man, normally so verbose.

"You are my son, Alan."

CHAPTER TWELVE

"MY father . . ." Alan groped for words, failed, became silent.

The Fireclown spread his large hands, his painted fool's face incongruous now.

"I was, in spite of anything you may have heard, much in love with your mother. We planned to marry, though Simon Powys wouldn't hear of it. I was a common space-pilot and she was Miriam Powys. That was before we could find the courage to tell him you were going to be born. We never did tell him —not together, anyway."

"What happened?" Alan spoke harshly, his heart thumping with almost overwhelming emotion.

"I got sent on a secret project. I couldn't avoid it. I thought

108

it would only last a couple of months but it kept me away for nearly two years. When I got back Simon Powys wouldn't let me near you—and your mother was dead. Powys said she'd died of shame. I sometimes think he shamed her into dying." The Fireclown broke into a laugh but, unlike his earlier laughter, this was bitter and full of melancholy.

Alan stood up, his body taut.

"What's your real name? What did you do? What did my grandfather say?"

The Fireclown ceased his laughter and shrugged his great shoulders.

"My real name—Emmanuel Blumenthal—Manny Bloom to my friends . . ."

"And fans," Alan said softly, remembering a book he'd had confiscated as a child. His grandfather had, meaninglessly he'd thought, taken it from him with no explanation. The book had been called *Heroes of Space*. "Manny Bloom, test pilot of the *Tearaway*, captain of the Saturn Expedition. That was the secret project, wasn't it? Saviour of Venus Satellite Seven."

"Co-pilot of the *Solstar* . . ." The Fireclown added.

"That's right—the *Solstar*, an experimental ship. It was supposed to have gone off course and crashed into the sun. You were reported dead."

"But a Martian freighter, carrying contraband so that it dare not notify the authorities or land in an official port, rescued us."

"Corso told me. That was ten years ago, as I remember. Why have you never contacted me? Why didn't you get custody of me when you came back from Saturn and found my mother was dead?"

"Simon Powys threatened to ruin me if I went near you. I was—heartbroken. Heartbroken—yes—but I reckoned you'd have a better chance than any I could give you."

"I wonder," Alan said gloomily. "A kid would have been happy just knowing his father was Manny Bloom—Commander Manny Bloom, frontiersman of space!" The last phrase held a hint of irony.

"I wasn't like the stories, though I thought I was when younger. I loved my own legend then, had it in mind nearly all the time. I wasn't naturally brave. But people behave as other people expect them to—I acted brave."

"And now you're the Fireclown, shouting and raving against
109

intelligence—championing mindless consciousness—with your fingerprints burned off, I suppose, and no records of who you really are. That's part of the general mystery solved, anyway. And part of my own—the main part."

"And now you know I'm your father, what will you do?"

"What can the knowledge possibly affect?" Alan said sadly.

"Your subconscious." The Fireclown grinned, half enjoying a private joke against his son.

"Yes, that, I suppose." He sighed. "What are you going to do?"

"I have work that holds me. Soon Corso, Cornelia and I will journey out beyond the Solar system in the *Pi-meson.* There I shall conduct certain experiments on my own mind and on theirs. We shall see what good intelligence serves—and what great good, I suspect, pure consciousness achieves. Do you want to come, Alan?"

Alan deliberated. He had no place with the Fireclown. There were things to sort out on Earth. He shook his head.

"It grieves me to see you reject a gift—maybe the greatest gift in the universe!"

"It is not a gift that suits my taste—father."

"So be it," the Fireclown sighed.

The *Solar Bird* soared down into Earth's atmosphere and streaked across oceans and continents before Helen switched on its braking jets and plunged into Hamburg spaceport.

The berth was ready for her and she steered into it. The water drained from the interior chamber.

Alan preceded her out of the airlock.

As he stepped into the chamber, a man entered through the other door.

"My God, Powys, where've you been?" It was Denholm Curtis, a mixture of worry and anger on his face.

Alan didn't answer immediately but turned to help Helen out of the ship. He didn't need the pause since he had already worked out his answer.

"We've been to see my father."

"Your father! I didn't know you . . ."

"I only found out who he was recently."

"I see. Well . . ." Curtis was nonplussed. "I wish you and Helen had told me."

110

"Sorry. We had to leave in a hurry. Your ship's perfectly all right."

"The ship's not important—it was you and Helen . . ." Curtis pursed his lips. "Anyway, I'm glad that's all it was. What with the threat of the Fireclown making an attack and everything, I thought you might have been kidnapped or killed." He smiled at his sister, who didn't respond. Helen had been silent for most of the trip. "But rumours about the pair of you are rife. Scandal won't do either of you any good—least of all Helen. Uncle Simon's popularity is rising incredibly. Overnight he's become the dominant man in Solar politics. You've got a tough fight on—if you still intend to fight."

"More than ever," Helen said quietly.

"I've got a car upstairs. Want to come back with me?"

"Thanks," they said.

As her brother lifted his car into the pale Hamburg sky Helen said to him: "What do you think of this Fireclown scare, Denholm?"

"It's more than a scare," he said. "It's a reality. How can we be sure he hasn't planted bombs all over the world—bombs he can detonate from space?"

Alan felt depressed. If Denholm Curtis, who rebelled habitually against any accepted theory or dogma, was convinced of the Fireclown's guilt then there was little chance of convincing anyone else to the contrary.

"But do you realize, Denholm," he said, "that we have only the word of one man—Simon Powys—and circumstantial evidence to go on? What if the Fireclown isn't guilty?"

"The concept's too remote for me, I'm afraid," Denholm said with a curious glance at Alan. "I didn't think anyone doubted the Fireclown had planned to detonate his cache. There were enough bombs there to blow the world apart."

"I doubt if he planned anything," Helen said.

"So do I." Alan nodded.

Denholm looked surprised. "I can understand you being uncertain, Helen, after your support of the Fireclown. It must be hard to find out you've been wrong all the way down the line. But you, Alan—what makes you think there could be a mistake?"

"There's the one big reason—that all the evidence against the Fireclown is circumstantial. He might not have known about the bombs, he might not have been responsible for the

111

holocaust that swept the levels. He might not, in fact, have had any plan to destroy anything at all. We haven't captured him yet, we haven't brought him to trial—but we've all automatically judged him guilty. I want to see my grandfather—he's the man who has convinced the world that the Fireclown is a criminal!"

Curtis was thoughtful. "I never thought I'd get caught up in hysteria," he said. "But, although I'm fairly sure the Fireclown is guilty, I admit there's a possibility of his being innocent. If we could prove him innocent, Alan, the war scare would be over. I'm already perturbed about that. You know the government has been approached by the arms syndicate?" This last remark to Helen.

"It's logical." Helen nodded. "And we've also considered the chance that this whole thing has been engineered by the dealers —not the Clown."

"That crossed my mind, too, at first," Denholm agreed. "But it seems too fantastic."

"Let's go and have this out with the Man of the Moment," Alan suggested. "Can you take us to grandfather's apartment, Denholm?"

"Take you? I'll come with you."

As the trio entered Simon Powys's apartment, they were greeted by Junnar.

"Glad to see you're both all right," he said to Alan and Helen. "Minister Powys is in conference with the President, Chief Sandai, Minister Petrovich and others."

"What's it about?" asked Alan, unwilling to be put off.

"The Fireclown situation."

"So that's what they're calling it now!" Alan said with a faint smile. "You'd better disturb them, Junnar. Tell them we've got some fresh information for them."

"Is it important, sir?"

"Yes!" Helen and Alan said in unison.

Junnar took them into the sitting room, where they waited impatiently for a few moments before he came back, nodding affirmatively.

They entered Simon Powys's study. The most powerful politicians in the Solar System sat there—Powys, Benjosef, gloomy-faced Petrovich, Minister in the Event of Defence, hard-featured Gregorius, Minister of Justice, smooth-skinned, red-cheeked Falkoner, Minister of Martian Affairs, and tiny,

112

delicate Madame Ch'u, Minister of Ganymedian Affairs. Beside the mantelpiece, standing relaxed and looking bored, was a man Alan didn't recognize. His eyes were at once amiable and deadly.

Simon Powys said harshly: "Well, Alan, I hope you've got an explanation for your disappearance. Where have you been?"

"To see the Fireclown." Alan's voice was calm.

"But you said . . ." Denholm Curtis broke in.

"I had to tell you something, Denholm. That was before I decided to come here."

"The Fireclown! You know his whereabouts?" Powys glanced at the tall man by the mantelpiece. "Why didn't you tell us immediately you knew?"

"I didn't know for certain until I found him."

"Where is he?" Powys turned to address the tall man. "Iopedes, be ready to get after him!"

"I met him in space," Alan said. "We went aboard his space-ship. He won't be in the same region of space now. He wouldn't let us go until he'd moved on."

"Damn!" Simon Powys got up. "We've got every ship of the three planets combing space for him and you discovered him, by chance. Did you learn anything?"

"Yes." Somewhere, in the last few actionful days, Alan had found strength. He was in perfect control of himself. He addressed the entire group, ignoring his fuming grandfather.

"I believe the Fireclown to be innocent of any deliberate act of violence," he announced calmly.

"You'll have to substantiate that, Mr. Powys," purred Madame Ch'u, looking at him quizzically.

"How do you know?" Simon Powys strode over to his grandson and gripped his arm painfully.

"I know because I spent some hours in the Fireclown's company and he told me he had nothing to do with the bomb plot or the burning of the levels."

"That's all?" Powys's fingers tightened on Alan's arm.

"That's all I needed," Alan said, and then in a voice which only his grandfather could hear: "Let go of my arm, grandfather. It hurts."

Simon Powys glared at him and released his grip. "Don't tell me you're still being gulled by this monster! Helen—you saw him, too—what did you think?"

"I agree with Alan. He says the policemen tampered with his
113

delicate flame-machines and that's what caused the holocaust. He says he knew nothing of the bombs. I suspect they were planted on him by the arms syndicate—in order to start the scare which you're now helping to foster."

"In short," Alan said, "I think this whole business has been engineered by the syndicate."

The room was silent.

Alan pressed his point. "I think you've all been blinded by the apparent discovery that the Fireclown wasn't what he at first seemed. Now you've turned completely against him—you believe him capable of any crime!"

"Mr. Powys"—Petrovich spoke with an air of assumed patience—"we are the government of the Solar System. We are not in the habit of jumping to ill-considered and emotional conclusions."

"Then you're not human," Alan said sharply. "Everyone can make mistakes, Minister Petrovich—especially in a heated atmosphere like this."

Petrovich smiled patronizingly. "We have considered the place of the arms syndicate in this business. We are sure they are taking advantage of the situation—but we are convinced that they did not 'engineer it', as you say."

Simon Powys roared: "My grandson's an immature fool! He has no understanding of politics or anything else. When the Fireclown lisps his innocence he believes him without question. Helen Curtis is just as bad. Both of them, to my own knowledge, were on the Fireclown's side from the start. Now they refuse to see the facts!"

The tall man, Iopedes, began to walk towards the door. Simon Powys called after him. "Iopedes—where are you going?"

"The young people said the Fireclown had left the area of space he was originally occupying. That could indicate he's gone to Mars or Ganymede. It's a better lead than we held, at any rate." Iopedes left.

"Who's he?" Alan said.

"Nick Iopedes, the ARP's top agent. He's been commissioned to bring the Fireclown to justice—by any means he has to employ."

"You're turning the system into a police state!" Helen said angrily.

"There's a state of emergency existing!" Simon Powys said

coldly. "The world—perhaps the Solar System—is threatened with destruction."

"In your mind and in the minds of those you've managed to convince!" Alan retaliated. "Have any bombs exploded? Has any threat been made?"

"No." This was Benjosef, who had hitherto seemed detached from the argument taking place around him.

"And the arms syndicate has approached you with a bargain, I hear." Alan laughed sharply.

"That is true," Benjosef agreed. Quite obviously, he was no longer in control of his cabinet. Simon Powys dominated it now, as if he had already superseded Benjosef. The old man seemed to accept the situation fatalistically.

"So there's your answer—the syndicate plant the bombs and start the scare. Then they sell you more bombs to 'defend' yourselves against a non-existent menace! Then what? Another scare—another move by the syndicate—until the seeds of war have been thoroughly planted. Everybody's armed to the teeth and the possibility of conflict between the planets is increased!"

"Oh, that's very pat," Simon Powys sneered. "But it doesn't fit the evidence. You know what you've done? You've been to see the Fireclown and instead of gaining information which could help us capture him, you've listened to his sweet protestations of innocence and thrown away a chance to help save the world!"

"Really?" Alan said in mock surprise. "Well, I disagree. It seems to me that *you* are taking the world to the brink of destruction, grandfather, by your blind hatred of the Fireclown."

"Leave, Alan!" Simon Powys's voice shook with anger. The assembled ministers look disturbed and embarrassed by what was, in the main, a family row.

Alan turned and walked out of the door, Helen following him. Denholm Curtis remained in the room, a frown on his face.

Outside, Helen smiled faintly. "Well, we seem to have antagonized everyone, don't we?"

"I'm *sure* we're right!" Alan said. "I'm certain of it, Helen. That trip the Fireclown took us on convinced me. He's too interested in his weird philosophizing to be capable of any plots against the system."

Helen took his arm.

115

"It's our opinion against theirs, I'm afraid."

"We've got to do something about convincing the ordinary people," Alan said as they descended the steps to the ground floor. "This is still a democracy, and if enough people protest they can be ousted from power and a more sane and rational party can solve the situation better."

"They're sane and reasonable enough," she pointed out. "They just don't happen to believe in the Fireclown's innocence."

"Then what are we going to do about it?"

She looked up at him. "What do you expect? I'm still in the running for President, Alan. I'm still leader of my party. We're going to try and win the election."

CHAPTER THIRTEEN

DIRECTOR Carson, head of City Administration, looked hard at Alan and nodded understandingly.

"It would be best if you resigned," he agreed. "Though, as far as it goes, you're the ablest assistant I've ever had, Alan. But with things as they are and with you outspoken against Simon Powys and for the Fireclown, I doubt if City Council would want you to stay on, anyway."

"Then we're both in agreement," Alan said. "I'll leave right away, if that's all right with you, sir."

"We'll manage. Your leave is due soon, anyway. We'll settle up your back-pay and send it to you."

They shook hands. They liked one another and it was obvious that Carson regretted Alan's leaving C.A. But he'd been right.

"What are you going to do now?" Carson said as Alan picked up his briefcase.

"I've got another job. I'm Helen Curtis's personal assistant for the Presidential campaign."

"You're going to need a great deal of luck, then?"

"A great deal," Alan agreed. "Goodbye, sir."

The Radical Liberal Movement Campaign Committee met at its headquarters. They sat round a long table in the large, well-lighted room. One of the walls comprised a huge laser screen—a usual feature of the windowless apartments in the City of Switzerland.

Helen sat at the head of the table with Alan on her right, Jordan Kalpis, her campaign organizer, on her left. The two heads of the RLMs' Press and Information Department sat near her—Horace Wallace, handsome and blank-faced, Andy Curry, small, freckled, and shifty-eyed—both Scots who had hardly seen Scotland and were yet anachronisms in their pride for their country. National feeling hardly existed these days.

Also at the table were Publicity Chief Mildred Brecht, an angular woman; Vernikoff, Head of Publications and Pamphlets; Sabah, Director of Research, both fat men with unremarkable faces.

Helen said: "Although you've all advised me against it, I intend to conduct my campaign on these lines. One,"—she read off a sheet of paper before her—"an insistence that other steps be taken to apprehend whoever was responsible for storing those bombs on the first level. Although we'll agree it's possible that the Fireclown was responsible, we must also pursue different lines of investigation, in case he was not. That covers us— the present policy of concentrating on the pre-judged Fireclown does not."

"That's reasonable," Sabah murmured. "Unless someone reveals that you personally believe the Fireclown innocent."

"Two,"—Helen ignored him—"that more money must be spent on interstellar space-flight research—we are becoming unadventurous in our outlook."

"That's a good one." Mildred Brecht nodded.

"It fits our 'forward-looking' image." Curry nodded, too.

"Three, tax concessions to Mars and Ganymede settlers. This will act as an incentive to colonizers. Fourth, price control on sea-farm produce. Fifth, steps must be taken to re-locate certain space-ports now occupying parts of the sea-bed suitable for cultivation . . ." The list was long and contained many other reforms of a minor nature. There were several short discussions on the exact terms to use for publicizing her proposed policy. Then the means of presenting them.

Mildred Brecht had some suggestions: "I suggest we can stick to old fashioned handbills for the main policy outline. World-wide distribution to every home on Earth. Large size talkie posters for display purposes. Newspaper displays for

117

Earth and the colonies . . ." She outlined several more means of publicizing the campaign.

Jordan Kalpis, a swarthy, black-haired man with prominent facial bones and pale blue eyes, interrupted Mildred Brecht.

"I think, on the whole, we're agreed already on the main points of Miss Curtis's policy as well as the means of publicizing them. We have a sound image, on the whole, and some nice, clear publicity material. The only troublesome issue is that of the Fireclown. I would like to suggest, again, that we drop it—ignore it. Already we have lost a lot of headway by the swing in public opinion from support to condemnation of the Fireclown. We can't afford to lose more."

"No," Helen said firmly. "I intend to make the Fireclown situation one of my main platform points. I am certain we shall soon find evidence of the Fireclown's innocence. If that happens, I shall be proved right. Powys proved the hysteric he seems to be, and public faith in me should be restored."

"It's too much of a gamble!" Kalpis insisted.

"We've got to gamble now," Helen said. "We haven't a chance of winning otherwise."

Kalpis sighed. "Very well," and lapsed into silence.

Alan said: "When's the first public speech due to be made?"

"Tomorrow." Helen fidgeted with the papers before her. "It's at the City Hall and should be well-attended."

The huge area of City Hall was packed. Every seat was occupied, every inch of standing space crammed to capacity. On the wide platform sat Alan, Helen, Wallace and Curry, staring out at the rows of heads that gaped at them from three sides. Behind them on a great screen pictures were flashed—pictures of Helen talking to members of the public, pictures of Helen with her parents, pictures of Helen visiting hospitals, old people's homes, orphanages. A commentary accompanied the pictures, glowingly praising her virtues, As it fininshed, Alan got up and addressed the crowd.

"Fellow citizens of the Solar System, in just a few weeks from now you will have voted for the person you want to be President. What will you look for in your President? Intelligence, warmth of heart, capability. These are the basic essentials. But you will want more—you will want someone who is going to lead the Solar Nation towards greater freedom, greater prosperity—and a more adventurous life. Such a woman is

Helen Curtis . . ." Unused to this sort of speech-making, Alan found he was quite enjoying himself. Enough of the Powys blood flowed in him, he decided, after all. He continued in this vein for a quarter of an hour and then presented Helen to the crowd. The applause was not as great as it might have been, but it was satisfactory.

Helen's platform manner was superb. At once alert and confident, she combined femininity with firmness, speaking calmly and with utmost assurance.

She outlined her policy. At this stage she ignored the Fireclown issue entirely, concentrating her attack on the sterile Solrefs and their Presidential candidate Simon Powys. She ignored hecklers and spoke with wit and zest.

When she finished she was applauded and Alan Powys got up, raising his arms for silence.

"Now that you have heard Miss Curtis's precise and far-thinking policy," he said, "are there any questions which you would like to ask her?"

Dotted around the auditorium were special stands where the questioner could go and be heard through the hall. Each stand had a large red beacon on it. Beacons began to flash everywhere. Alan selected the nearest.

"Number seven," he said, giving the number of the stand.

"I should like to ask Miss Curtis how she intends to work out the controlled price of sea-farm produce," said a woman.

Helen went back to the centre of the platform.

"We shall decide to price by assessing cost of production, a fair profit margin, and so on."

"This will result in lower prices, will it?" the woman asked.

"Certainly."

The red light went out. Alan called another number.

"What steps does Miss Curtis intend to take towards the present ban on tobacco production?"

"None," Helen said firmly. "There are two reasons for keeping the ban. The first is that nicotine is harmful to health. The second is that land previously used for tobacco is now producing cereals and other food produce. Marijuana, on the other hand, is not nearly so habit-forming, has fewer smokers and can be produced with less wastage of land."

There were several more questions of the same nature, a little heckling, and then Alan called out again: "Number seven-nine."

119

"Miss Curtis was an ardent supporter of the Fireclown before it was discovered that he was a criminal. Now it's feared that the Fireclown intends to bombard Earth from space, or else detonate already planted bombs. What does she intend to do about this?"

Helen glanced at Alan. He smiled at her encouragingly.

"We are not certain that the Fireclown is guilty of the crimes he has been accused of," she said.

"He's guilty all right!" someone shouted. A hundred voices agreed.

"We cannot condemn him out of hand," she went on firmly. "We have no evidence of a plot to attack or destroy the planet."

"What would you do if he *was* guilty," shouted the original speaker—"sit back and wait?"

Helen had to shout to be heard over the rising noise of the crowd.

"I think that the Fireclown was framed by unscrupulous men who want a war scare," she insisted. "I believe we should follow other lines of investigation. Catch the Fireclown, by all means, and bring him to trial if necessary. But meanwhile we should be considering other possibilities as to how the bombs got on the first level!"

"My parents were killed on the eleventh level!" This was someone shouting from another speaking box. "I don't want the same thing to happen to my kids!"

"It's sure to unless we look at the situation logically," Helen retaliated.

"Fireclown-lover!" someone screamed. The phrase was taken up in other parts of the hall.

"This is madness, Alan." She looked at him as if asking for his advice. "I didn't expect quite so much hysteria."

"Keep plugging," he said. "It's all you can do. Answer them back!"

"Powys for President! Powys for President!" This from the very back of the hall.

"Powys for insanity!" she cried. "The insanity which some of you are exhibiting tonight. Blind fear of this kind will get you nowhere. I offer you sanity!"

"Madness, more likely!"

"If you listened to me like sensible adults instead of shouting and screaming, I'd tell you what I mean." Helen stood, her arms folded, waiting for the noise to die down.

Alan went and placed himself beside her.

"Give her a chance!" he roared. "Give Miss Curtis a chance!"

When finally the noise had abated somewhat, Helen continued:

"I have seen the Fireclown since the holocaust. He told me that policemen tampered with his machines and caused the fire. He had nothing to do with it!"

"Then he was lying!"

"Calm down!" she begged. "Listen to me!"

"We listened to the Fireclown's lies for too long. Why listen to yours?"

"The Fireclown told you no lies. You interpreted what he said so that it meant what you wanted it to mean. Now you're doing the same to me! The Fireclown is innocent!"

Alan whispered. "Don't go too far, Helen. You've said enough."

She must have realized that she had overshot her mark. She had been carried away by the heat of the argument, had admitted she thought the Fireclown innocent. Alan could imagine what the lasercasts and news-sheets would say in the morning.

"Are there any other questions?" he called. But his voice was drowned by the angry roar of the crowd.

"Not exactly a successful evening," he said as he took her home. They had had to wait for hours before the crowd dispersed.

She was depressed. She said nothing.

"What's the next stage in the campaign?" he asked.

"Next stage? Is it worth it, Alan? I'm getting nowhere. I've never known such wild hysteria. I thought we got rid of all that a century ago."

"It takes longer than a hundred years to educate people to listen to reason when someone tells them their lives are liable to be snuffed out in an instant."

"I suppose so. But what are we going to do? I didn't expect such a strong reaction. I didn't intend to say that I thought the Fireclown was innocent. I knew that was going too far, that they couldn't take direct opposition to what they now believe. But I got so angry."

"It's just unfortunate," he said comfortingly, though inwardly he was slightly annoyed that she had lost her self-control at the last minute. "And it's early days yet. Maybe, by the time the campaign's over, we'll have more people on our side."

"Maybe they'll just ignore us," she said tiredly as they entered her apartment.

"No, I don't think that. We're nothing if not controversial!"

Next day, the RLM Political Headquarters received a deputation.

Two men and two women. The men were both thin and of medium height. One of them, the first to advance into the front office and confront Alan, who had elected to deal with them, was sandy-haired, with a prominent Adam's apple and a nervous tic. The others were less remarkable, with brown hair and a mild face in which two fanatical eyes gleamed. The women might have been pretty if they had dressed less dowdily and paid more attention to their hair and make-up. In a word, they were frumps.

The taller woman carried a neat banner which read: THE END OF THE WORLD DRAWS SLOWLY NIGH. LATTER-DAY ADVENTISTS SAY 'NO' TO FALSE GODS. STOP THE FIRECLOWN.

Alan knew what they represented. And he knew of the leader, had seen his face in innumerable broadcasts.

"Good morning, Elder Smod," he said brightly. "What can we do for you?"

"We have come as the voice of the Latter-Day Adventists to denounce you," Elder Smod said sonorously. The Latter-Day Adventists were now the strongest and only influential religious body in existence today, and their ranks were comprised so obviously of bewildered half-wits and pious paranoiacs that public and politicians alike did not pay them the attention that such a large movement would otherwise merit in a democracy. However, they could be a nuisance. And the main nuisance was Elder Smod, second-in-command to senile Chief Elder Bevis, who was often observed to have fallen asleep during one of his own speeches.

"And why should you wish to denounce me?" Alan raised his eyebrows.

"We've come to denounce the Radical Liberal Movement for its outrageous support of this spawn of Satan, the Fireclown!" said one of the frumps in a surprisingly clear and musical voice.

"But what have the Latter-Day Adventists to do with the Fireclown?" Alan asked in surprise.

"Young man, we oppose the supporters of Satan."

"I'm sure you do. But I still don't see what connection . . ."

"Satan seeks to destroy the world by fire before the good Lord has his chance. We cannot tolerate that!"

Alan remembered now that the original twentieth-century sect had announced that they were the only ones who would be saved when the world was destroyed by fire. They had been a little chary of announcing the date but, egged on by slightly disenchanted supporters, they had finally given an exact date for the end of the world—2,000 A.D., claiming the Third Millennium would contain only the faithful. Sadly, when the Third Millennium dawned, it contained fewer of the faithful than before, since many had not wholly accepted the fact pointed out to them by the movement's elders, that the Bible had earlier been misread as to the date of Christ's birth. (A speedy and splendid juggling with the Christian, Jewish and Moslem calendars had taken place on January 1st, 2,000 A.D.). But, in spite of the discredit, the movement had grown again with the invention of a slightly altered interpretation—i.e., that the world would not perish in a sudden holocaust but that it would begin —and *had* begun—to perish from the year 2,000—giving an almost infinite amount of time for the process to take place. However, the coming of the Fireclown scare, with its talk of destruction, had evidently thrown them out again!

"But why, exactly, have you come to us?" Alan demanded.

"To ask you to side with the righteous against the Fireclown. We were astonished to see that there were still foolish sinners on Earth who could believe him innocent! So we came—to show you the True Way."

"Thank you," said Alan, "but all I say—and I cannot speak for the RLM as a whole—is that the Fireclown is *not* likely to destroy the world by fire. We have no argument."

Elder Smod seemed a trifle nonplussed. Evidently he considered the Fireclown a sort of johnny-come-lately world-destroyer, whereas his movement had had, for some time, a monopolistic concession on the idea.

Alan decided to humour him and said gently: "The Fireclown could be an agent for your side, couldn't he?"

"No! He is Satan's spawn. Satan," said Smod with a morose satisfaction, "has come amongst us in the shape of the Fire-clown."

"Satan? Yet the clown predicted a return of fire to the world unless, in your terms, the world turned its back on Mammon. And one cannot worship both . . ."

"A devil's trick. The Fireclown is Satan's answer to the True Word—*our* word!"

It was no good. Alan couldn't grasp his logic—if logic there was. He had to admit defeat.

"What if we don't cease our support of the Fireclown?" he asked.

"Then you will be destroyed in the flames from heaven!"

"We can't win, can we?" Alan said.

"You are like the rest of your kind," Elder Smod sneered. "They paid us no attention, either."

"Who do you mean?"

"You profess not to know! Ha! Are you not one of that band who call themselves the Secret Sons of the Fireclown?"

"I didn't know there was such a group. Where are they?"

"We have already tried to dissuade them from their false worship. A deputation of our English brothers went to them yesterday, but to no avail."

"They're in England? Where?"

"In the stinking slums of Mayfair, where they belong, of course!" Elder Smod turned to his followers. "Come—we have tried to save them, but they heed us not. Let us leave this gate-way to Hell!"

They marched primly out.

Mayfair. Wasn't that where Blas had his hideout? Perhaps the two were connected. Perhaps this was the lead that would prove, once and for all, whether the Fireclown planned mammoth arson or whether the syndicate had framed him.

Alan hurriedly made his way into the back room where Helen and Jordan Kalpis were planning her tour.

"Helen, I think I've got a lead. I'm not sure what it is, but if I'm lucky I'll be able to get evidence to prove that we're right about the Fireclown. He's still got some supporters, I just learned, in London. I'm going there."

"Shall I come with you?"

"No. You've got a lot of ground to make up if you're going to get near to winning this election. Stick at it—and don't lose your self-control over the Fireclown issue. I'll get back as soon as I've got some definite information."

"Alan, it's probably dangerous. Blas and his like take pains to protect themselves."

"I'll do the same, don't worry," he said. He turned to Kalpis. "Could we have a moment, Jordan?"

Jordan walked tactfully out of the room.

Alan took Helen in his arms, staring down at her face. She had a half-startled look, half-worried. "Alan . . ."

"Yes?"

She shook her head, smiling. "Look after yourself."

"I've got to," he said, and kissed her.

CHAPTER FOURTEEN

MAYFAIR mouldered.

Nowhere on the three planets was there a slum like it, and riches, not poverty, had indirectly created it.

As Alan walked up the festering streets of Park Lane, a light drizzle falling from the overcast afternoon sky, he remembered the story of how it had got like this. Mayfair was the property of one man—a man whose ambition had been to own it, who had achieved his ambition and was now near-senile—Ronald Lowry, the British financier, who refused to let the government buy him out and refused, also, to improve his property. The original residents and business houses had moved out long since, unable to stand Lowry's weird dictatorship. The homeless, and especially the criminal homeless, had moved in. Like Lowry, they weren't interested in improving the property, either. For them, it was fine as it was—a warren of huge, disused hotels, office blocks and apartment buildings. Lowry was rich—perhaps the richest man in the world—and Lowry, in spite of his senility, had power. He would not let a single government official set foot on his property and backed up his wishes by threatening to withdraw his capital from industries which, without it, would flounder and give the government unemployment problems, re-location problems and the like. Until a less cautious party came to power, Mayfair would continue to moulder, at least for as long as Lowry lived.

The scruffy, old-world architecture of the Hilton, the Dorchester and the Millennium Grande towered above Alan as he passed between them and the jungle that grew alongside Hyde Park. Hyde Park itself was public property, neat and orderly, well maintained by London's City Council, but roots had spread and shrubs had flowered, making an almost impenetrable hedge along the borders of the park.

Wisely, he did not head immediately for the Dorchester, where Blas was supposed to be, but went instead to a café that still bore the name of the Darlington Grill. The *specialité de la maison* these days, however, was fish and chips—from the smell.

The majority of the men were gaudily dressed in the latest styles, but some were down at heel—not necessarily criminals, but pridies, people who refused to accept the citizen's grant which the government allowed to all who were unable to work, whether because of physical or emotional reasons. These were extreme emotional cases who, if they had not come to the official-free area of Mayfair, would have been cured by this time and rehabilitated. Mayfair, Alan thought, was indeed a strange anachronism—and a blot on the three planets. Ronald Lowry's vast financial resources had produced the only skid-row now in existence!

Alan had taken the precaution of getting himself a green luminous suit and a flowing scarlet cravat which made him feel sick whenever he saw himself in a mirror. On his head was perched, at a jaunty angle, a conical cap of bright and hideous blue, edged with gold sateen.

He saw by the list chalked on a board at the end of the café that his nose hadn't lied. The only food was turbot and chips. The liquor, it seemed, was a product of a local firm—a choice between wheat, parsnip or nettle wine. He ordered a wheat wine and found it clear and good, like a full-bodied Sauterne. It was only spoiled by the disgusting aroma of illicit cigarettes smoked by several of the nicotine addicts who lounged in what was evidently a drug-induced euphoria at the greasy tables.

Before he had left the City of Switzerland, Alan had procured one of the badges previously worn by the Fireclown's supporters—a small metal sun emblem which the disillusioned Sons of the Sun had rid themselves of when public sympathy for the Fireclown had changed to anger. He wore it inside his cap.

126

He looked around over the rim of his glass, hoping to see a similar emblem, but he was disappointed.

A sharp-faced little man came in and sat at Alan's table. He ordered a parsnip wine. A few drops spilled on the table as the proprietor brought it.

Alan decided that he would have to chance the possibility that the café fraternity were sufficiently angered against the Fireclown to cause trouble. He took off his hat, lining upward so that the sun emblem was visible.

The sharp-faced man was also sharp-eyed. Alan saw him stare at the badge for a moment. Then he looked at Alan, frowning. In the spilled liquor on the table he drew, with a surprisingly clean finger, a similar design.

"You're one of us, eh?" he grunted.

"Yes."

"Fresh to Mayfair?"

"Yes."

"You'd better come to the meeting. It's a masked meeting, naturally. We've got to protect ourselves."

"Where do I go?"

"South Audley Street—a cellar." The man told him the number and the time to be there. Then he ignored Alan, who finished his drink and ordered another. A little later he got up and left.

Alan could understand the need for secrecy. The police would be searching for any clue to the Fireclown's whereabouts. He wondered if this group knew. Or did they have any real contact with the Fireclown at all? Perhaps in an hour's time, at six o'clock, he would know.

At six he entered the broken-down doorway in South Audley Street and found himself in a long room that had evidently been a restaurant. Through the gloom he could make out chairs still stacked on tables. He walked over rotting carpets, through the piled furniture to the back of the place. A door led him through a filthy, dilapidated kitchen. At the end of a row of rusted stoves he saw another door. Opening it, he saw that it closed off a flight of concrete steps leading downwards. He advanced into a cellar.

About five or six masked figures were already there. One of them, stocky and languid in his movements, Alan thought he recognized.

One of the others, a woman in a red and yellow hood that

covered her whole face, came up to him. "Welcome, new-comer. Sit there." She pointed to a padded chair in a shadowed corner.

From a brazier at the end of the cellar flames danced. Huge, grotesque shadows were spread along the floor and up the walls as the men and women began to come down the cellar steps and sit on the damp-smelling chairs.

"Thirty-nine, plus the newcomer—forty in all," the stocky man said. "Close the door and bar it."

The stocky man went and stood by the brazier. Alan wished he could place him, but couldn't for the moment.

"We are come here," he intoned, "as the last loyal Sons of the Fireclown, to honour our leader and prepare for his return. We are pledged to carry out his work, even if we risk death in so doing!"

Alan realized suddenly that these people were using the Fire-clown's name, just as the majority had done earlier, to support some creed or obsession of their own. The whole tone of the meeting did not fit with what he knew of the Fireclown, his father. Probably, he thought, he understood the Fireclown bet-ter than anyone—particularly since he could recognize certain traits in the Fireclown that had a milder expression in himself.

Certainly, he decided, this group was worth observing, for it might help clarify the rest of the questions that needed clarify-ing before he could act in an objective way.

What if the arms syndicate were operating this group for their own purposes? It was possible that they had got hold of these people who seriously wished to put the Fireclown's *outré* philosophy into practive and were making them act against the Fireclown's interests.

Then he had it. The identify of the intoning man—*Blas!*

Now, he felt, there was substance for his theory that the arms syndicate was using the Fireclown as a patsy—a fall-guy to carry the can for their devious plans for the world conflict. He bent forward as Blas came to the important point.

"You have each been given incendiary bombs to plant in some of the major buildings around the globe. The burning buildings will act as beacons, heralding the return of the Fire-clown with his bolts of fire for the unclean and his gift of a new world for you, the true believers. Are you all sure of what you must do?"

"Yes!" each man and woman responded.

128

"Now." Blas's masked face was cocked to one side as he suddenly regarded Alan. "The newcomer is not yet a full Son of the Fireclown. He must prove himself to us."

Alan suddenly realized the menace in the words. He sensed, from the atmosphere in the room, that this was not normal procedure.

"Come here, my friend," Blas said quietly. "You must be initiated."

There was a strong chance that Blas recognized him. But what could he do? For the moment he would have to go through with it.

He got up slowly and walked towards the fiery heat of the brazier.

"Do you worship the Flame of the Sun?" Blas asked theatrically.

"Yes," he said, trying to keep his voice level.

"Do you see the fire as the Fire of Life?"

He nodded.

"Would you bring forth the fires of life in yourself?"

"Yes."

"Then"—Blas pointed at the brazier—"plunge your hand into the flames as proof that you are a brother to the Flame of the Sun!"

Ritual! If Alan needed confirmation that these people had nothing to do with the Fireclown in any real sense, he had it now. The Fireclown scorned ritual.

"No, Blas," he said scornfully, and turned to the masked gathering. "Don't listen to this man. I know the Fireclown— he is my father—he would not want this! He would hate you to debase yourselves as you are doing now. The Fireclown only uses fire as a symbol. He speaks of the human spirit, not—" he gestured at the brazier—"natural fire!"

"Silence!" Blas commanded. "You seek to disrupt our gathering! Do not listen to him, brothers!"

The Sons of the Fireclown were glancing at one another uncertainly.

Blas's voice spoke almost good-humouredly in Alan's ear. "Really, Powys, this is nothing to you. Why do you interfere? Admit to these fools that you lied and I'll let you go. Otherwise I can probably convince them, anyway, and you'll be roasted on that thing there."

Alan glanced at the blazing brazier, gouting flames. He shuddered. Then he leapt at it and kicked it over in Blas's direction. Blas jumped away from the burning coals, shouting something incoherent.

Alan pushed through the confused crowd and reached the door, wrenched the bar away and fled up the steps. He ran through the darkened restaurant and out into the crumbling street a few seconds ahead of his closest pursuer. He dashed down towards Grosvenor Square, an overgrown tangle of trees and shrubs. In the last of the evening light he saw the monolithic tower of the old American Embassy, fallen into decay long since.

A flight of steps led up to the broken glass doors. He climbed them hurriedly, squeezed through an aperture and saw another flight of steps leading upwards.

By the time he had reached the second floor, let his feet lead him into a maze of corridors, he no longer heard the sounds of pursuit and realized, thankfully, that he had lost them. He cursed himself for not wearing a mask. He should have guessed that Blas and the suspicious Sons of the Fireclown had some connection.

And now it was almost certain that Blas, unknown to the Fireclown, was playing both ends against the middle. But he'd still have to find out more before he could prove the Fireclown's innocence.

He had only one course of action. To go to the Dorchester, where Blas had his hideout. He knew he wasn't far from Park Lane, since he had studied a map thoroughly before he left. He waited for two hours before groping his way down to a different exit from the one he'd left and stumbled through the jungle of Grosvenor Square, climbing over fallen masonry and keeping in the shadows as he walked down Grosvenor Street and into Park Lane.

He threw away his hat and reversed his jacket as an afterthought so that the reversible side showed mauve shot with yellow, hunched his shoulders to disguise his outline and hid his face as much as possible, then continued down towards the Dorchester.

Luckily, the street was almost deserted and he passed only a couple of drunks sitting against the wall of a bank, and a pretty young girl who hailed him with pretty old words. She reviled him softly in language even older when he ignored her.

Reaching the side entrance of the Dorchester, he found the

door firmly locked. He continued round to the front. Lights were on in the lobby and two tough-looking men lounged outside. He couldn't get past them without them seeing him, so he walked boldly and said:

"I've come to see Mr. Blas—he's expecting me. Which suite?"

"First floor," said the guard unsuspiciously.

Alan found the lobby in surprisingly good repair. Even the elevators looked in working order, although there was a good deal of litter about. He took the stairs, reached the first floor, which was in semi-darkness, and saw a light coming from under a pair of big double doors. He paused outside and strained his ear to catch the mumble of voices from within. He was sure he recognized both of them—one was probably Blas's, anyway.

The other, he realized after a moment, was the voice of Junnar, his grandfather's secretary!

He took from his pocket the squat laser pistol he had brought with him at Helen's request and walked into the room.

"The plot," he said with forced lightness, "thickens. Good evening, gentlemen."

Blas took the cigarette out of his mouth with an expression of surprise. "Good evening, Powys," he said amiably. "I didn't think we'd seen the last of you. If you're not going to be impetuous we can explain everything, I think."

"Mr. Powys," Junnar said sadly, "you should have stayed out of this from the start. What's the gun for?"

"Self-protection," Alan said curtly. "And I don't need much explanation. I've had an inkling of this for some time. Grandfather put you up to planting the bombs on the Fireclown—am I right?"

Junnar's silence was answer enough. Alan nodded. "He'd use any means to prove the Fireclown a criminal, even if it meant supplying the proof himself, in a very simple way. You got the bombs from Blas and planted them. But you bit off more than you could chew when you started this war scare. What are you up to now? Doing another deal with Blas over the arms he wants to supply the government with as a 'defence' against a non-existent plot?"

"That's about it," Blas admitted.

Alan felt physically sick. His own grandfather, head of the house of Powys, descendant of a line of strong, honest and fervently dedicated politicians, had descended to faking evidence

131

to prove his own theory about the Fireclown. And, in consequence, he had started a wave of hysteria which he was virtually unable to control. He wondered if Simon Powys now regretted his infamy. He probably did, but it was too late.

And this was the man the public were almost bound to elect President.

"You bloody, treacherous pigs!" he said.

"You'd have to prove all this," Blas said softly, his self-assurance still apparently maintained.

Alan was still in a quandary. All his life the concept of clan loyalty to the Powys's had been drummed into him. It was hard to shake it off. Could he betray his own grandfather, who in a peculiar way he still loved, at the expense of the father responsible for his bastardy?

Slowly, standing there with the laser gun in his hand, its unfamiliar grip sticky with sweat, he came unwillingly to a decision.

He waved the gun towards the door. "After you," he said.

"Where are we going?" Junnar asked nervously.

"The City of Switzerland," Alan told them. "And just remember what a laser can do. I could slice you both in two in a moment. It's going in my pocket, and my hand's going to be on it all the way."

"You're rather a melodramatic young man," Blas said resignedly as he walked towards the door.

CHAPTER FIFTEEN

UNDER Alan's direction, Junnar brought the car down on the roof of the Powys' apartment block.

"Climb out, both of you," Alan ordered. They obeyed him.

They descended to Simon Powys's apartment and Junnar made the door open. They went through.

"Is that you, Junnar?" Powys called from his study.

Alan herded them in.

He saw a terrible expression of sheer fear cloud his grandfather's face as they entered.

Hollowly, Alan said: "I know everything, grandfather."

Simon Powys remained seated at his desk. Slowly he put down his stylus and pushed the papers from him.

"What are you going to do then, Alan?"

"Denounce us, I expect," Blas said cheerfully. "May I sit down, Powys?" He turned to Alan.

"Both of you sit," Alan ordered, his hand still on his pocketed gun.

"You'd have to prove it," Simon Powys said slowly, in an old man's voice. "It's the word of an emotional young man against that of a respected minister. I could say you were raving. Neither Junnar nor Blas would testify against me."

"Why?" Alan demanded. "Why, grandfather?"

"There are a number of reasons, Alan. It was my last chance to become President. A Powys of every generation has been President at least once. I couldn't let family tradition die —it would have been a disgrace."

"Isn't what you did a disgrace? Isn't it a crime?"

"You don't understand. Politicians can't always use clean methods. I was right. The Fireclown's no good, Alan. It was the only way to show the public . . ."

"That was only a matter of opinion. The fact is you framed the Fireclown in order to prove your own theory about him— and because Helen was bound to win the election if you didn't do something desperate. It was the only way to change public opinion radically. Because of that, Sandai's police tampered with the Fireclown's flame machines—and three hundred people were killed."

"I didn't want that to happen."

"But it happened—*you* were responsible for their deaths!"

"I feel guilty . . ."

"You *are* guilty! And you fell neatly into Blas's plan, didn't you? He supplied you with the bombs with which you framed the Fireclown. And now, because you daren't admit the whole thing was manufactured by you, he's holding the government up to blackmail. There is a possibility of mass destruction if this hysteria builds up—but even if that doesn't happen the money that Blas will demand will impoverish Sol for years. And he's got you neatly in his trap—he can dictate any terms he wants. If you were elected President you would be his puppet. Blas would run Sol. And he nearly succeeded, didn't he?"

"As your grandfather pointed out," Blas said equably, "you still have to prove all this, young man."

"I intend to, Blas. Grandfather—you're going to confess, before it's too late. You're a Powys! You must!"

133

Simon Powys wet his lips and stared down at the desk.

"Are you going to confess, grandfather?"

"No," said Simon Powys. "No, I am not."

It had been Alan's only chance, and it had failed. As his grandfather and Blas had said, it was his word against theirs. Already he had the reputation as a die-hard supporter of the Fireclown. Who would believe him now that Simon Powys had turned the Solar System against the Fireclown? What could he do now?

His idealism, his belief that his grandfather would act in accordance with the principles he had so plainly shed was shattered. He was drained of emotion and could only stand staring down at the old man.

"Stalemate, Powys." Blas crossed his legs.

There must be proof, Alan thought. There must be proof somewhere.

He knew that if he could prove his grandfather's guilt he could stop Blas's plan for controlling the Solar System, avert the threat of a war almost bound to come about with so much hysteria in the air, prove the Fireclown innocent and allow Helen to become President.

Everything hinged on what was, in fact, a means of betraying his grandfather.

He gave Blas a disgusted glare.

"Yes, stalemate. But if I walk out of here now, you daren't do anything for fear that I'll say too much. You can't rig evidence against me the same way as you did to the Fireclown." As an afterthought, he added: "You could kill me, of course."

"No!" Simon Powys rose from his chair. "Alan, come in with us. In a few weeks the world will be ours!"

Alan went towards the door. "You accused me once of having none of the noble Powys blood, remember? If that's what flows in your veins, thank God I haven't got any!"

He flung down the gun and left.

Outside, he walked slowly towards the elevator cone, brooding and unable to think coherently. All he had was definite knowledge of his grandfather's perfidy, knowledge that he was unable yet to prove. Still, the knowledge itself was something.

He went down to the thirtieth level and made his way to the RLM Headquarters.

134

He entered the front office, still stacked with posters. Jordan Kalpis was there, his bony face full of worry.

"Powys! What did you find out?"

"Where's Helen? I'll tell you later."

"At a meeting in the Divisional Hall on forty. There's some pretty bad heckling going on. The crowd has turned nasty."

"Right. I'm going over there."

Alan went out into the corridor and took the fastway to the elevator, rose ten levels and took the fastway again to the Divisional Hall. Every ten levels had a Divisional Hall, comprising a meeting hall and the offices of the local sub-council officials. Outside, the posters of Helen had been torn down.

There was a fantastic noise coming from inside. Alan entered the crowded hall and glimpsed Helen at the far end on the platform. A man beside him threw back an arm. Alan saw it held a piece of raw meat. As the man's hand came up to hurl the meat, Alan grabbed it and wrenched it savagely back. He didn't give the man time to see who had stopped him but pushed his way down the aisle. All kinds of refuse was flying on to the platform as he hauled himself up.

Helen's face was bleeding and her clothes were torn. She stood rigidly, defiantly shouting at the mob.

"Helen!"

She saw him. "Alan! What—?"

"Get out of here—they're not listening to you!"

She seemed to pull herself together.

Now the mob surged forward, faces twisted, hands grasping. He heard someone shout: "She wants us burned to death."

She—wants—us—burned—to—death!

A gem of a phrase, Alan thought as he kicked the first man who tried to climb the stage. It fed the hysteria which spawned it. He found himself hating humanity and his kicks were savage.

Andy Curry's freckled face appeared from the side exit. "Quick! Here!"

They ran in and Curry ordered the door locked.

"I can only say I told you so," Curry said dourly. "You shouldn't have made the speech in the first place, Miss Curtis."

"I avoided all mention of the Fireclown," she said furiously, "and they didn't give me a chance!"

Curry picked up the phone in the passage. He pressed two studs.

The word *Police* flashed on the screen and an operator's face followed it.

"I'm speaking from Divisional Hall, level ten," Curry said swiftly. "There's a riot going on down here. We're besieged. We need help."

The operator looked at him. "Helen Curtis meeting—is that right?"

"That's right."

"We'll have a squad there right away," the operator told him in a voice that indicated he should have known better than to start trouble.

The police dispersed the crowd and the captain told Alan, Helen and Curry that an escort was ready to see them home. He sounded unsympathetic, as if he was helping them unwillingly.

When they reached Helen's door the leader of the escort said: "If I were you, Miss Curtis, I should stay inside. You're liable to be attacked otherwise."

"I've got an election to fight," she pointed out.

"You'll have people to fight if tonight's trouble's repeated —and I don't doubt it will be if you insist on setting yourself up to resist the whole climate of public opinion! We've got enough on our hands with the Fireclown investigation— crowds demanding to know when we're going to catch him, rabble-rousers shouting that we must prepare for war, and all the rest of it."

The escort leader shrugged. "We can't be held responsible if you deliberately risk being mobbed."

"Thank you, officer." Alan followed Helen into the apartment. The door closed.

"So I'm supposed to stay boxed in here, am I?" she said bitterly. "Meanwhile I've got to try and convince people that they're wrong."

"It's useless," he said hollowly, going into the sitting-room and slumping down in a chair.

"What did you find out in London?"

"Everything."

"Even what Blas is up to?"

He told her, slowly and wearily, all that had happened.

"So we were right," she said thoughtfully. "But uncle Simon —that's incredible."

"Yes, isn't it?" He smiled cynically. "And our hands are virtually tied. We've got to do some cool thinking, Helen."

She was calmer now. She seemed to notice, for the first time, that he was exhausted.

"We'd better sleep on it," she said. "We may feel more optimistic in the morning."

As they breakfasted, Alan switched on the laser. "Let's see what's happened in the world this morning," he said.

". . . petition urging the government to speed up its defence plans," mouthed the newscaster. Then he leaned forward urgently. "For those who missed our early edition, the first attacks by the Fireclown have begun! Two nuclear bomb explosions have been observed—one in the Atlantic and one in the Gobi Desert. So far nobody has been reported hurt, but it will be impossible to know for certain for some time yet. Where will the Fireclown's next bomb strike? Swiss City? New York? Berlin? We don't know. Emergency shelters are being erected and bomb detector teams are covering the areas around the main cities to try and discover hidden bombs. Meanwhile, in Britain, mystery fires have devastated important public buildings. The National Gallery is smouldering wreckage—the marvellous architectural beauty of Gateshead Theatre is no more. Precautions are being taken to protect other such buildings throughout the planet. There is little doubt that the Fireclown—or his die-hard supporters here—was reponsible!"

"That's all Blas's work," Alan said angrily. "How are we going to prove it?"

"Look," Helen pointed at the screen, Simon Powys had appeared, looking dignified and grave.

"My fellow citizens of the Solar System, I am speaking to you in troubled times. As I predicted a short while ago, the Fireclown has attacked the globe. He has been offered no hostility, we have intended him no harm. But never-the-less he has attacked. We must defend ourselves. If we had to manufacture bombs and other weapons for defence we should be wiped out before we had any chance. Luckily the Solar government has been offered arms." Powys paused as if saddened by the task he had to perform. "A group of men— criminals we should have called them but a few hours ago, but now we are more than thankful to them—have offered us a supply of arms. We are going to purchase them, on your

137

behalf, and set them up around the planet. This will have to be done swiftly, and already bodies of volunteers are working on emergency installations. Let us hope we shall be in time to avert our peril. When I next speak to you, perhaps we shall know."

"The devil!" Helen swore. "He's obviously completely in Blas's power. He knows that Blas will use him to control Earth—that we're threatened with a military dictatorship, and yet, in his pride, he still refuses to stop. Doesn't he know what he's doing?"

"He's gone so far now that he can't go back. His hate for the Fireclown and love for his own political ambitions have combined and, in a sense I'm sure, turned him insane! Maybe he can't even see the extent of his treachery."

"We've got to do something to stop him, Alan." Helen spoke quietly.

"Like what?"

"First we'll try to convince Sandai. Then, if that fails, we'll have to kill him."

"Helen! Killing him won't do any good. What could we do? Set up another dictatorship to control the people? Don't you see that if we continue this violence we'll breed more violence *ad infinitum?* We've *got* to use legal means against him. Otherwise, society as we know it is finished!"

"Then what other alternative is there?"

"First we'll see Sandai," he said. "Then we'll decide."

CHAPTER SIXTEEN

IT took time to get to see Sandai. It took over a day. By the time they walked into his office they were looking very tired indeed. So was Sandai.

"If you've come to tell me that the Fireclown's innocent of these outrages," he said, wiping his olive forehead, "I'm not interested."

Alan stood over the seated police chief, his hands resting on the man's desk.

"That's part of it, Chief Sandai. But that's not all. I have heard the man responsible confess his guilt to me!"

"You've what?" Sandai looked up, astonished.

"The man responsible for framing the Fireclown, for setting off the bombs and causing the fires in Britain, is a man named Blas."

"Blas? François Blas? He's suspected head of the arms syndicate." Sandai looked thoughtful. "It's a possibility, Mr. Powys. But what proof have you? How did you find out?"

"I heard that Blas had his headquarters in Mayfair. I went there and discovered he was running an organization calling themselves the Sons of the Fireclown."

"So Blas is working for the Fireclown?"

"No. The thing was definitely spurious. Blas was using it for his own ends. Later I broke into Blas's apartment and confronted him with what I knew and what I suspected. He denied nothing. He told me to prove it—which I couldn't do. I then brought him and another man back to the capital . . ."

"Who was the other man?"

"Junnar, my grandfather's secretary."

"You mean you suspect he's been working against Minister Powys? That's fantastic—if it's true."

"He's been working *with* Powys," Alan said firmly. "Blas and my grandfather are hand-in-glove—they plan to use the war scare they've created and the fear of the Fireclown to hold the Earth to ransom. You heard yesterday's announcement—about Powys having to buy bombs from the syndicate. It's a set-up, Chief Sandai!"

"Young man, you're evidently deranged." Sandai stood up and patted Alan's arm sympathetically.

"Listen to him!" Helen said urgently. "Listen, Chief Sandai. It sounds impossible, but it's a fact."

"And the proof?" Sandai said gently.

"As circumstantial as that against the Fireclown," Alan pointed out.

"But the Fireclown is a renegade—your grandfather is virtually the leader of the Solar System. That's the difference, Mr. Powys. I'm sorry, but your defence of the Fireclown doesn't hold up. Why don't you admit that and work with the rest of us to avert the menace?"

"It's the truth," Alan said. He felt the energy go out of his body, his shoulders slump.

"I'm very busy," Sandai said. "You'd better leave now."

As they crossed the sunny gardens of the Top, Helen said to him: "That didn't work. What do we do now, Alan?"

139

"Watch the world die," he said hopelessly.

"The whole lot of them deserve death for what they're doing," she said cautiously.

"Maybe. But the law banished the death sentence over a hundred years ago. We want to preserve the law, Helen, not demolish it further!"

"If only we could contact the Fireclown. Maybe he could help us."

"He's journeying off somewhere in that ship of his, conducting his experiment. There's no hope there, anyway. He's not interested in Earth's problems, you know that."

They reached the elevator cone and entered it with a dozen others.

As they descended a man stared hard at Helen.

"Aren't you Helen Curtis?" he said roughly.

"I am."

The man spat in her face.

Alan jumped at him, punching savagely. The attendant shouted for them to stop. Hands grabbed Alan. The man punched him in the stomach and then in the head.

"Stinking fire-bug!"

Alan felt bile in his throat. Then he passed out.

He came to in a few seconds. The lift was still going down. Helen was bending over him. The lift stopped. "You'd better get out, both of you," the attendant said.

Alan got to his feet.

"Why?" he grunted.

"You're making trouble, that's why."

"We didn't start it."

"Come on, Alan," Helen said, taking his arm. "We'll walk."

He was weak with pain as they stumbled into the corridor. Also he was insensately angry.

She helped him on to the fastway and supported his weight until his strength returned.

"That shows you how much anything we say is worth," she said quietly. "Hatred and violence are everywhere. What harm would a little more do? The good would outweigh the bad, Alan."

"No," he gasped. "No, Helen. Simon Powys sold his principles. I'm not selling mine."

"So," she said when they were back in her apartment, "what do we do? Just wait here and watch the world collapse?"

140

"Switch on the set so we've got a good view," he said. She went over and turned on the laservid.

They watched glumly as the announcer reported another explosion in the Pacific, two more in Central Africa, killing a large number of people who lived in small communities in the blast area. Work was under way on the defence project. Simon Powys was directing the preparations.

"They don't need to bother with the farce of electing him," Helen said. "He's as good as President now!"

"You mean Blas is," Alan told her. "He's the one pulling the strings."

Helen reached over to the laser and pressed out a number.

"Who are you calling?"

"My brother," she said. "Denholm's about the only person who can help us now."

Her brother's face came on the screen. "Hello, Helen, I'm rather busy—is it important?"

"Very important, Denholm. Could you come over?"

"If it's another defence of the Fireclown . . ."

"It is not."

Her brother's expression changed as he stared at her image. "Very well. Give me an hour—all right?"

"Okay," she said.

"How can Denholm help us?" Alan said. "What's the point?"

"We'll tell him all we know. The more people of importance who are told about it, the better chance we have."

Denholm came in, placed his gaudy hat on a chair arm and sat down.

"Alan," Helen said, "tell Denholm everything—from the time we went to see the Fireclown until our interview with Sandai."

He told Denholm Curtis everything.

When he had finished, Curtis frowned at him. "Alan," he said, "I think I believe you. Uncle Simon's been behaving a trifle mysteriously in some ways. The alacrity with which he managed to contact the dealers when the government finally decided to buy the arms was astonishing. It could mean that he's abused his position as chairman of the One Hundred Committee!"

"What do you mean?"

"Supposing in some way he had got hold of a list of the

dealers and the location of their caches? Supposing he held on to it without letting the other committee members know, contacted Blas and concocted this scheme? Suppose then they worked out a plan to take advantage of the Fireclown, get Simon Powys elected as President, and then run the world as they wanted to run it? Powys might have got in touch with Blas originally with a view to smashing the syndicate. But Blas might have proposed the whole idea. We all know how much uncle Simon hates the Fireclown. It would have been the perfect means of getting rid of him. Maybe he intended to capture the Fireclown. Maybe the original deal was simply over a few bombs. But Blas has provided the Fireclown with the means of producing a super-ship, and he was fairly certain that the Fireclown would escape when the chips were down. He did. The war scare started, aided by the police tampering with the flame-machines. Simon Powys couldn't back out—and Blas had him where he wanted him."

"That sounds logical," Alan agreed.

"But all this needs proof to back it up." Denholm Curtis pursed his lips thoughtfully.

"It comes back to that every time." Helen sighed.

"There'd be only one way. To find the man who was Powys's original contact with Blas, and get him to confess."

"But how?" Alan asked. "Where do we look?"

"We check the files of the One Hundred Committee—that was probably how Powys found his contact. You're still secretary, Helen. Where are the files?"

"Right here. In the safe."

"Get them."

She got them—dozens of spools of microfilm. They fitted them into the projector.

It was more than six hours before they found what they were looking for. A reference to one Nils Benedict, suspected of trying to sell arms to a super-reactionary Crespignite splinter group. They had turned him over to the police. The police had been unable to find any evidence against him. Simon Powys had interviewed him while in custody and reported that, in his opinion, the man was innocent. Simon Powys had been, apart from the police, the only man to question Benedict. Benedict had a Brussels address.

"Do you think that's him?" Alan said, rubbing his eyes.

"It's the only one it could possibly be. What do we do now?"

"Pay Nils Benedict a visit, I suppose," Helen suggested.

A smaller, less complex version of the City of Switzerland, Brussels had an altogether different character. Every inch of stonework was embellished with red lacquer, and over this bright designs had been laid. Gilt predominated.

The structure rose fourteen levels above the ground, five below, covering an area of five square miles. The roof landing space was limited so that they were forced to land outside the city and take a mono-rocket which let them off on the tenth level. Benedict lived on level eight.

They reached his apartment. They had already decided that Denholm would do the talking, since he was less likely to be suspect that the other two.

"Nils Benedict," he said to the blank door, "this is Denholm Curtis. I've got some good news for you."

The door opened. A tall, rangy man in a dressing gown of green silk stared curiously at Curtis.

"Are you from Powys?" he asked as the door closed behind them.

Alan took the lead. "We want to contact Blas in a hurry. Can you arrange it?"

"Sure. But why? I thought he was in direct contact nowadays."

That was enough. Now they knew for certain.

"Oh, he is," Alan said. "But we thought it would be nice for you and Simon Powys to meet again after all this time."

Benedict had been uncommonly slow, he thought, for a man who was supposed to live by his wits. The man seemed gradually to realize that something was wrong. He backed into his living room. They followed.

The answer was there. Benedict was an addict. The stink of mescaline was in the room; nightmarish murals covered the walls. He was a mescamas who got his kicks from descending into his own psychological hell.

Helen said in a strained voice: "I'll wait outside."

"Come on, Benedict," Denholm said roughly.

"I have right, you know," Benedict said thickly. "Why does Powys want to see me?"

"Are you scared of Powys?"

143

"He told me I'd be killed if I ever got in touch with him again."

"There's not a chance of that, I promise," Alan said.

Benedict was still wary. Alan suddenly hit him under the jaw. He collapsed.

"Let's get him dressed," Denholm said. "It wouldn't be proper for him to go out without his correct clothes on."

They had surprisingly little difficulty getting Benedict to Helen's apartment. Organization of the usual kind seemed to have gone to pieces during the fake emergency.

While Helen tried to revive Benedict and Denholm tied his hands, the laser began to flash. Alan answered it. Chief Sandai looked out at him.

"You're not the only madman in the system, it seems," he said. "I thought about what you told me and thought I couldn't do any harm to assign a few men to go undercover to Mayfair and check your story. It held up. We found Blas and Junnar there. We're holding them, under the emergency laws which Simon Powys insisted we make, as suspects in an arson plot. We got one of the Sons of the Fireclown, too. But we're going to need more proof—and I'm still not convinced that your tale about Simon Powys is true!"

Alan stepped aside so Sandai could see Benedict.

"Recognize this man, Chief?"

"I've got a feeling I do, but I can't place him. Who is he?"

"He's Simon Powys's original contact with Blas. He's a mescamas. If we withhold his supply for a short time he should tell us everything he knows."

"If it's true, you've had a big stroke of luck, young man."

"It'll be the first we've had," Alan said dryly. "Can you come over and pick us up? It might be wise to have an escort."

Sandai nodded. The screen blanked.

Blas alone remained seemingly at ease. Benedict was slumped hopelessly in his chair, perhaps even enjoying the experience of defeat. Junnar had his back to them, staring out of the window over the mountains. The police prison had a wonderful view.

Blas said: "Chief Sandai, what evidence do you have for these fantastic charges? Confront Simon Powys with them. He will laugh at you!"

Sandai turned to Denholm Curtis. "Where's Powys now? You've convinced me."

"He's at a special meeting in the Solar House. Members are asking him questions on his war policy. He's bound to answer since we still retain a vestige of democracy."

"What are you going to do, Chief?" Alan asked.

"Something spectacular," Sandai said. "It's probably the only thing we can do now to break Powys's power in front of the assembly. Otherwise it may be too late."

"After what I've been through in the last day or so," Helen said grimly. "I'm beginning to doubt that anyone can topple uncle Simon!"

Standing nobly before the mighty assembly of Solar Representatives, Simon Powys answered their questions in a grave and sonorous voice. He was the image of the visionary and man of action. The weight of responsibility seemed to rest heavily upon his broad shoulders, but he bore it manfully, not to say hypocritically.

Alan watched him on the screen outside the main entrance to the Assembly Chamber itself. He, Denholm and Helen stood in a group to one side. Chief Sandai, four policemen and the fettered trio of Junnar, Blas and the slobbering Benedict stood to the other.

They choose their moment well, when a member for Afghanistan asked Simon Powys what the police were doing in the Fireclown investigation.

Sandai pushed the button operating the double doors. The doors swept open and the party pushed forward.

"The police," Sandai called, "have caught most of the men responsible for the present situation." He gestured dramatically towards the shackled men. "Here they are—there is only one man missing!"

Alan saw that Simon Powys's face bore an expression similar to the look he'd had on the night he'd accused him.

But he held up well, Alan decided, considering everything.

"What does this interruption mean, Chief Sandai?"

Sandai spoke laconically. "Using the emergency powers vested in me by the government of the Solar System I am holding under arrest the three men you see there—François Blas, suspected arms dealer, Nils Benedict, a contact for the arms syndicate—and Eugene Junnar, personal assistant to Minister Simon Powys. All the men admit to being implicated

145

in a plot, instigated by Minister Powys, to frame the Fireclown, start a war scare by means of nuclear bomb explosions and incendiaries, and thus assure Minister Powys of full political power as President of the Solar System!"

Blas said: "He's lying, Minister Powys."

But Nils Benedict, not of Blas's calibre, continued the theme. "We didn't admit anything, sir! I haven't said a word about the deal!"

Simon Powys thundered: "Be quiet! You have abused your powers, Sandai. I demand that you leave the hall immediately!"

But the hubbub from the rest of the representatives drowned out anything else he might have wished to say.

Alan walked swiftly down to the central platform and mounted it.

"We have witnesses, now, grandfather! We have the proof you told us to get!"

Benjosef rose from his seat.

"What's the meaning of this, Mr. Powys?"

"My grandfather, sir, has betrayed every trust you and the system have ever put in him." Briefly, Alan outlined the facts.

Benjosef turned to Simon Powys who stood rigidly, as if petrified, in his place. "Is this true, Powys?"

"No!" Powys came alive, his face desperate—wretched. "No! Can't you see this is the work of the Fireclown's supporters, an attempt to disgrace me and confuse us in our hour of peril? My grandson is lying!"

But Simon Powys had lost all self-control. His wild denial had convinced the assembly of his guilt. He knew it. He stared around him, his breathing irregular, his eyes wide. He advanced toward Benjosef.

"I run the Solar System now, Benjosef—not you! You can't do anything. The people are with me!"

"Possibly," Benjosef said mildly, with a slight air of triumph, "but evidently this assembly is not." Benjosef seemed pleased at his would-be successor's downfall. "I was aware, Minister, that you wished to oust me as President—but I did not expect you to take quite so much trouble." He gestured to the police chief. "Sandai—I'm afraid you had better arrest Minister Powys."

Simon Powys leapt from the dais, stumbled and fell. He got up, evidently in pain, and stood there panting as Sandai stepped cautiously towards him.

"You fool! I could have made the world a better place. I knew it was going soft. I could have stopped the rot! You are under my orders, Sandai—don't listen to Benjosef."

Sandai slipped a pair of electrogyves from his belt.

"No!" Simon Powys was sobbing now. "The Fireclown will destroy us! He will destroy you all—as he destroyed my daughter!"

Alan looked up in surprise. So his grandfather had known all along that the Fireclown was his father! That explained, even further, his insensate hatred of the Fireclown.

He went up to the old man, pitying him now.

"Grandfather, I know you have suffered, but . . ."

Old Simon Powys turned his great head and looked into Alan's eyes. His expression was that of a bewildered, tearful child.

"It was for her sake," he said brokenly. "For hers and yours, Alan."

The gyves hummed and curled about Powys's wrists. His head bowed, his seamed face now tear-streaked, he allowed Sandai to lead him out of the assembly hall.

Benjosef stepped from the platform and touched Alan's arm. "I'm sorry you had to do what you did, my boy. I must admit I never liked your grandfather—always thought him, well, somewhat weak, I suppose. That was why I, and many members of the party, never promoted him to a more prominent position; why he had never, until now, been nominated as a Presidential candidate. Evidently I was right, at least." He turned to Helen Curtis. "The world is going to be grateful to you both, I suspect. The climate of opinion is going to take yet another reversal before the elections are finally held. I hope you make a good President, Miss Curtis."

"Thank you, sir," said Helen, looking worriedly at Alan.

Alan ran a hand across his face. He swallowed with difficulty and glowered at the ground. Then he shook Benjosef's hand off his arm.

"I'm glad you're all proved right," he said bitterly. "I'm bloody glad about the happy ending."

And he walked straight up the aisle and out of the Solar Hall, his pace fast as he crossed the lawns. His heart pounding, his eyes warm, his fists clenched and his mind in a mess.

CHAPTER SEVENTEEN

TWO days later Alan emerged from the cavern on the first level, where he had been avoiding everyone, and ascended to the Top, passing a great many talkie-posters proclaiming Helen Curtis for President. Listening to the conversation, his faith in the stupidity of human nature was fully restored. In the swift movement of events, the public had changed their loyalty from the Fireclown to Simon Powys, and now to Helen Curtis. Why did they need heroes? he wondered. What was wrong in people that they could not find what they needed within themselves? How did they know Helen was any better than the rest?

News-sheets announced the complete rounding up of the members of the arms syndicate and the discovery of every nuclear cache left in existence. That was one good thing. The news-sheets also said that order had been completely restored. Alan wondered. On the surface, perhaps, it was true. But what of the disorder that must still exist in the hearts and minds of most members of the public?

He reached the Top and entered Police Headquarters. After a few moments he was shown into Chief Sandai's office.

"Mr. Powys! There has been a general search out for you! You and Miss Curtis are the heroes of the hour. Every laservid station and news-sheet in the Solar System has been after you."

"In that case," Alan said coolly, "I'm glad they couldn't find me. I want to see my grandfather, Chief—if that's possible."

"Of course. He made a full confession, you know. He's been very subdued since his arrest—hasn't given us any trouble."

"Good. Well, can I see him now?"

Not exactly every home comfort had been provided for Simon Powys, but his room hardly looked like a prison cell with its pleasant view of the clear summer sky, the cloud-wreathed mountain peaks in the distance. It was well furnished. There were books, writing materials and news-sheets on the small desk by the window.

His grandfather was staring out at the mountains, his chair pushed back from his desk, when Alan entered.

"Grandfather."

The old man turned. And it *was* an old man who stared gauntly up at his grandson. All the vitality had left him. He seemed completely enervated.

"Hello, Alan. Glad to see you. Do sit down." He gestured vaguely towards the only other chair in the room.

"How do you feel?" Alan asked inanely.

Simon Powys smiled thinly. "As well as can be expected," he said. "How are you?"

Alan seated himself on the edge of the chair. "I'm sorry I had to do it, grandfather, but you know why it was necessary."

"Yes. I'm glad, in a way, that you did—though I can hardly bear the shame. I don't know if you'll understand, Alan, but I *was* insane, in a way. I was caught up in a nightmare—my ambition, my hatred, my schemes ran away with me. Do you know that when my fortunes turned after the Fireclown business I seemed to be living in a dream thereafter? I feel as if I've just woken up. I remember I accused you of having none of the good Powys blood. I shouldn't have done that, and I'm sorry. I tried, in my way, to apologize almost as soon as I'd said it. But it seems you had better stuff in you than I. I've always been conscious of my inherent weakness, that I wasn't of the same breed as our ancestors, but I always fought it, Alan. I tried not to let it get the better of me. It did, of course, but in a different way."

"You didn't really hate the Fireclown for anything he was doing, did you?" Alan spoke softly. "You hated him for loving my mother, and giving her a son—me. You knew he was Manny Bloom all the time."

"Yes." Simon Powys sighed and stared out of the window again. "I knew he was Manny Bloom. I was responsible for sending him on the Saturn mission. That was my first major mistake, I suppose. But I couldn't see my daughter marrying an ordinary spaceman, however much of a hero he was in the public eye. I didn't realize you were going to be born. He was away for two years. When he came back you were here—and your mother had killed herself."

"Killed herself! I didn't know . . ."

"I'd told her Manny Bloom was dead—killed in a space accident. I didn't expect those consequences, of course. That was the first death I was responsible for, indirectly. As Minister for Space Transport I was in the perfect position to send

149

Manny Bloom wherever I chose. I bided my time—then I really *did* try to kill him."

"What? You mean the rocket that went too near the sun?"

"Yes. I bribed the technician responsible for the final check —had him fix the steering rockets so that the ship would plunge into the sun. I heard the ship had gone off course and I thought I was rid of him. But somehow he survived—and he came back, to haunt me as it were, as the Fireclown."

"So you really created your own nemesis. You caused my father to drift towards the sun and that experience resulted in his strange mental state. Ultimately he appeared as the Fireclown and, because of your hatred against him, brought about your ruin without ever consciously wishing for vengeance against you."

Simon Powys nodded. "I appreciate the irony of it all," he said. "It's one of the things I've been thinking about, sitting here and waiting for my trial."

"When is it to be?"

"They haven't fixed it yet. It's going to be a big one—will probably take place after the Presidential elections."

"Helen will be able to influence the judges then," Alan said. "She'll probably try to get you the lightest possible sentence."

"The lightest sentence would be death, Alan. And that, I'm afraid, is outside even the President's powers to exact."

Alan remembered Helen's proposal to assassinate Simon Powys. In many ways, he thought, everyone would have welcomed it. It was painful to see this once respected and powerful man in such a wretched state, no matter how much he deserved it.

Simon Powys got up, extending his hand. "It was good of you to come, Alan. I wonder if you would mind leaving now. This—this is somewhat hard to . . ." He broke off, unable to express his shame.

"Yes, of course." Alan went forward and shook Simon Powys's hand. The old man tried to make the grip firm, but failed.

Feeling considerably more affection for his grandfather than he had ever had in the past, Alan left the cell, left Police Headquarters and stood for a long time by a splashing fountain, staring into the clear water and watching the darting goldfish swimming in the narrow confines of the pool. Did they understand just how narrow their little universe was? he wondered. They seemed happy enough, if fish could be happy. But if they weren't happy, he reflected, neither were they sad. They had no tradition but instinct, no ritual but the quest for food and a mate. He didn't envy them much.

CHAPTER EIGHTEEN

IN the following weeks Alan led a fairly solitary life, taking little interest in the elections, scarcely aware of the fact that Helen was almost certain to win since there were no candidates in the field with her popularity. Denholm Curtis, who had played some part in the denunciation of Powys, was now the Solref's candidate for the office, but he didn't stand much of a chance. Helen was busy, but she had tried to contact him from time to time. He would see her when he was ready.

The election date came. The votes were counted. Helen was President.

The day after her election she came to see him and he let her in.

"I thought you were angry with me," she said as she accepted a drink. "I thought, perhaps, you'd decided not to see me again. I know you've had a bad series of emotional shocks, Alan—but I could have helped you. I could have been some comfort, surely."

"I didn't need comfort, Helen. I needed to be alone with myself. And anyway, you couldn't have afforded to waste time on me—you had problems of your own."

"What do you propose to do now?" She couldn't disguise the fact that she was anxious.

"Ask you to marry me, Helen."

"I accept," she said thankfully. "I thought . . ."

"We all tend to see other people's emotions as reflecting on ourselves. It's a mistake. People's emotions are rarely created by anyone else. I think we might be happy, don't you?"

"In spite of my work?"

"In spite of that, yes. I don't expect to see much of you for some time. But maybe that's for the best."

A buzz began to sound on her wrist.

"I'm sorry." She smiled. "I get issued with this thing—I'm

151

on call, as it were, all the time. I didn't expect it to start so soon."

She went to his laservid and pressed a number.

"President Curtis," she said to the slightly perturbed looking man on the screen. She put the drink down on the set.

"Madame—there is probably no danger but I have just received news that a strange space-ship has landed somewhere near Algiers. It's believed to be the Fireclown's."

"No need for declaring a state of emergency now." She smiled. "It will be good to see him again." She switched out and turned to Alan. "He's your father—want to be part of a deputation?"

"If it's just the two of us, yes."

"Come on then. Let's see what his experiments have proved."

Before Helen could go she was forced to leave notification of her whereabouts. Her Presidential duties had not really begun as yet, but from now on her time would never be her own. In his new state of mind, Alan decided he could bear it so long as she only served one term.

The *Pi-meson* rested on its belly, its pitted hull gleaming in the African sun. As yet, nothing had been heard from the ship. It was as if it was empty, bereft of life.

As their car settled beside it, the huge airlock began to open. But nothing else happened.

"What now?" Helen looked to Alan for guidance.

"Let's go in," he said, leading the way over to the ship and clambering into the airlock.

On the big landing deck Alan touched the stud operating the sliding wall. It opened and they climbed into the control deck. It was darkened. No light passed the closed ports.

"Father?" Alan spoke into the silence, certain someone was here. "Fireclown?"

"Alan . . ." The voice was rumbling, enigmatic, thoughtful.

"Yes—and Helen Curtis. We've got something to tell you." He was slightly amused at his decision to announce his engagement formally to his strange father.

A single light shone now from the corner. Alan could just make out the slumped bulk of the Fireclown. A short distance away Cornelia Fisher stirred. Corso seemed prone, but Alan thought he heard him mumble under his breath.

"Is anything wrong father?"

"No." The Fireclown raised his huge body up from the

152

couch. His gaudy tatters curled about him, his conical hat still bobbed on his head and his face was still painted. He chuckled. "I thought you'd come here first. I wouldn't have admitted anyone else."

"Helen and I are getting married, father."

"Ah . . . really?" The Fireclown didn't sound very interested. His manner had become, if anything, more detached and alien.

"A lot's been happening on Earth, sir," Helen put in, "since we last met. You're no longer an outcast."

The Fireclown's body shook with laughter which he at first suppressed and then let roll from his mouth in roaring gusts. "No—longer—an—outcast. Ha! Ha! Ha! Good!"

Nonplussed, Alan glanced at Helen, who frowned back at him.

"It is not I who am the outcast, young lady—not in the cosmic sense. It is the human race, with their futile, worthless *intelligence*."

"I still don't understand . . ." Helen said bewilderedly.

"I took you to the heart of the sun—I took you even to the heart of the galaxy and you still failed to understand! Consciousness is not the same as intelligence. Consciousness is content to exist as it exists, to be what it is and nothing more. But intelligence—that is a blot on the cosmos! In short, I intend to wipe out that blot. I intend to destroy intelligence!"

"Destroy intelligence? You mean, destroy life in the Solar System!" Alan was horrified.

"No, my son, nothing so unsubtle. For one thing, human life is the only culprit—the only thing that offends against the law of the universe. I have journeyed throughout the galaxy and have found nothing like it anywhere else. Intelligence, therefore, is a weed in the garden of infinity, a destroying weed that must be dealt with at once."

"You are mad!" Alan said desperately. "It's impossible to destroy intelligence without destroying those who have it!"

"According to human logic, that is true. But according to my logic—the Fireclown's logic—that is false. I have perfected a kind of fire—Time Fire, call it—which will burn away the minds of those it strikes without consuming them in body. My Time Fire will destroy the ability to think, because thought takes time."

The Fireclown reached out his hand towards a stud and depressed it. The wall hummed down. He went over to the controls and began to operate them. "I waited for you to arrive because I still retain some human sentiment. I did not want to make my son go with the rest. I will convince you, anon, that I speak truth and you will agree with me. You will want only consciousness!"

Alan strode towards his father and grasped his huge arm. "It can't work—and even if it could, who are you to take such a task upon yourself?"

"I am the Fireclown!"

The screen in front of them showed that the ship had once again set up its own peculiar field. The spheres began to flash past.

"See those!" The Fireclown pointed. "They are chronons—Atoms of Time! Just as there are atoms of matter, the same is true of time. And I control those atoms as ably as the physicists control their electrons and protons. They are the stuff of my Time Fire!"

Astounded, Alan could only believe his father. He turned to Corso, who was opening his eyes, a dazed look on his red face. "Corso! Do you want any part of this? Stop him! Cornelia"—the woman stared at him blankly—"tell him to cease!"

The Fireclown put his painted, bellowing face close to Alan's. "They cannot understand you. They hear you—but they hear sound alone! They are the first to gain from the Time Fire. They are fully aware but they have no intelligence to mar their awareness."

"Oh, God!" Helen looked aghast at the blank-faced pair.

"Where are we going?" Alan yelled at his insane father.

"I intend to put the ship into a time-freeze. Then, as the globe passes beneath me, I will unleash the Time Fire, covering the world with its healing flames!"

"No, father!"

"Don't try to tamper with the controls, Alan. If you do you will disrupt the time field and we might well perish."

The spheres—the chronons—flashed past. Alan stared at them, fascinated in spite of the danger. Atoms of Time. He had heard the chronon theory before, but had never believed it had any reality in fact. But there was no other explanation he could think of for the Fireclown's ability to ignore the laws of matter and venture into the sun's heart, travel swiftly through the galaxy to its centre and remain unharmed. Un-

154

harmed bodily, at least. His mind had obviously been unable to stand up against the impressions it had seen.

Faster and faster the chronons rolled past on the screen.

Concentrating on his controls, the Fireclown ignored them.

"What are we going to do, Alan?" Helen said. "Do you think he's right about this Time Fire?"

"Yes. Look at Corso and Cornelia for proof. He is a genius —but he's an idiot as well. We've got to stop him, Helen. Heaven knows what destruction he can work—even if it isn't as bad as he boasts!"

"How!"

"There's only one way. Destroy the controls!"

"We could be killed—or frozen forever in this 'time freeze' of his!"

"We've got to take the risk."

"But what can you do? We've no weapon, nothing to destroy them with!"

"There's one thing we can do. I'm going to grapple with him. He's incredibly strong so I won't be able to hold him for long. While I keep him occupied, go to the control panel and press all the studs, change the position of all the levers, twist all the dials. That should do something. Ready?"

Conscious that this might be the last time he saw her before they perished, he gave her a long, eloquent look. She smiled.

He leapt at the Fireclown's back and got his arm around his father's thick neck.

The great arms went up and the hands closed over his wrists. The Fireclown shook him off.

"I've spawned a fool! You could cause us to slip into a time vortex we could never get out of!"

Alan grabbed the Fireclown's legs and, surprisingly, though the clown was still a trifle off-balance, pulled him down.

Helen dashed towards the controls and began depressing studs and pulling levers.

"No!"

The Fireclown raised himself on one elbow, his other hand outstretched in a warning gesture.

The light began to fizz, to change colour rapidly. The ship shuddered. He was blinded by the glare, his head ached. He felt the Fireclown move and flung himself at his father. With a movement of his arm and body the Fireclown shook him off again.

Then the deck seemed to vanish and they seemed to hang in space. All around him now Alan saw the spheres whirling. The great chronons, each the size of the moon, spun in a dazzling and random course.

The Fireclown bellowed like a baleful bull from somewhere. He heard Helen's voice shouting. He could make no sense of their words. He tried to move but his body was rigid, would answer none of his commands.

Then the chronons changed colour and began to expand.

They burst! A chaotic display of coloured streamers smeared themselves all around him and dissipated swiftly.

Alan tried to breathe but couldn't.

Instead, he sucked in water!

It took seconds for him to realize that he was under the sea. He struggled upwards and at last reached the surface, drew air into his lungs. He was in the middle of an ocean, no land in sight.

There was no evidence that a ship had crashed. Had it entered the water so smoothly that it hadn't made a ripple?

But—another thought came—he should have been *in* the ship! How had he got out?

Another head broke the surface. He swam towards it. The Fireclown! The paint streaked his face. He was panting and cursing. Then Helen's head came up!

"What happened!" Alan gasped. "Father—what happened?"

"Damn you! You broke the time field—I've lost my ship!"

Overhead Alan heard the drone of an air-car. He looked up, waving frantically. It was an amphibian and it seemed to be looking for them. It came down low and landed.

Puzzled faces stared out of the cabin. Someone emerged on to the small, flat deck and a line flashed out over the water. Alan caught it, swam towards Helen and handed it to her. She was pulled swiftly in and, once aboard, the line was sent back. Alan handed it to the Fireclown.

The man refused to take it. Automatically, he kept himself afloat, but his face had an expression of melancholic suffering.

"Take it, father!"

"Why should I? What purpose do I fulfil by continuing to live? I have failed."

Impatiently, Alan tied the rope around the passive Fireclown and watched the great bulk being towed in. The Fire-

156

clown made no move to release himself or help himself on to the deck.

Alan took the line as it came out once again.

"How did you know we were here?" he asked the vessel's captain.

"We saw a peculiar kind of explosion in this area. We thought we'd better investigate. Sorry it took us so long. We've been circling over this area for three hours. Can't think how we missed you the first time."

"Three hours! But . . ." Alan stopped. "What time is it now?"

The captain glanced at his chronometer. "Fourteen hundred, almost."

Alan was about to ask the date but he decided against it. It seemed that they had been deposited in the ocean exactly half-an-hour before they entered the Fireclown's ship. But what had happened to the ship? he asked the morose Fireclown who had slumped himself moodily in a corner of the cabin.

"I told you—you broke the time field. What happened was simple—we existed in a different time location, the ship in another. The ship should make its appearance between now and the next million years!"

Thereafter, his father refused to answer further questions.

CHAPTER NINETEEN

THE trial of Simon Powys and the trial of the Fireclown were held at the same time, but in different courts. The laservid stations and the news-sheets were torn between which should have most prominence.

The *Pi-meson* had been found, intact, in Wyoming. Scientists had already stripped it of its time mechanisms and were investigating them. The Fireclown offered them no help when asked.

The relationship between the late protagonists came out, and scandal blended with sensation to feed the news-sheets and laservid networks.

Simon Powys was not very entertaining, however. He admitted all charges and was found guilty on all charges. Even

157

the judge did not exercise that strange prerogative which judges seem to think themselves entitled to—his summing up contained no list of his personal biases. It was quick and clean. Simon Powys was banished to a confined bunk in one of the pressure domes in the asteroid belt.

The Fireclown was more verbose, his case harder to try since it had no precedent. He could not be tried for his philosophical beliefs, or even for his unique intentions to destroy intelligence. The charge, when it was finally decided, read: "Plotting to disrupt human society to a point where it could no longer function."

His long speeches in his defence—or rather in defence of his creed—agreed with the charge.

"I am the victim of crude intelligence," he told the bewildered jury. "Intelligence which has no business to exist in the universe. I have been pulled down by it as it will pull down the human race in time. I tried to help you but, for all your vaunted minds, you could not understand. Perish, then, in spirit. Set yourselves against the law of the universe! Your punishment will come soon enough and be well merited!"

Though still puzzled, the jury decided the Fireclown's own punishment soon enough. They found him guilty but insane. He would be sent to a mental hospital on Ganymede.

Meanwhile, the scientists continued to puzzle over his bizarre equations and could arrive at no conclusion. In time, perhaps, they would, for once on the track they would never leave it.

For the time being, public hysteria died down, and society once again settled into an ordered existence. Helen Curtis began to put her reforms to the assembly and they were accepted or rejected after discussion. Progress would be slow and would always follow behind the demands of the reformers, but at least in this manner it might retain its dynamism. Helen was comparatively satisfied.

Their wedding date was fixed.

And then came the final drama.

Alan, once more looking for a job, scanned the list of specialist agencies, and sipped coffee. The laservid buzzed and he switched it to receive. Helen's face appeared on the screen.

"Alan—the Fireclown's escaped!"

He put down his cup with a clatter. "What! How?"

"You know how strong he was. He overpowered a guard, got hold of his gun and held up the entire Police Headquarters.

158

He made them release uncle Simon and they left in a stolen police car together."

"Where have they gone?"

"We don't know."

"I'm coming over. Are you at the House?"

"Yes."

When he reached the Presidential apartments Helen and some of her advisers were staring at the huge wall-screen. A commentary boomed:

"Our cameras have succeeded in tracking the escaping space-ship *Pi-meson*, containing convicts Manny Bloom, better known as the Fireclown, and Simon Powys!"

Deep space. The ship in clear focus.

"The ship, degutted of its weird time devices but retaining its ordinary drive, has so far outdistanced all pursuers."

"That answers my question," Alan said from behind Helen. "Where are they going?"

"They seem to be heading for Venus. They could just about survive there and certainly escape the police. The revitalization project is two-thirds complete."

"A strange pair to be travelling together," Helen reflected.

"They've got things in common," Alan pointed out. "In their different ways they were both reactionary idealists. They wanted things simpler than they in fact are."

The ship passed Venus.

"Where in the universe are they heading for?" Helen said, baffled.

Alan thought he knew.

He watched helplessly as the ship carrying his father and grandfather plunged on.

"Perhaps it's for the best—for them and for us," he whispered.

The *Pi-meson* passed the orbit of Mercury.

They watched as it wheeled and sailed in towards the sun.

It vanished, consumed almost immediately, as it followed its unveering course into the heart of Sol.

The watchers were silent. Helen turned her face up towards Alan and studied his expression. She glanced back at the screen.

In a few short weeks a new Age had come to Earth and gone as swiftly. It had left a strange mood behind it—and perhaps a new science. Sociologists and psychologists attempted to explain the sudden ebb of hysteria that had seized the people. There were a dozen theories, all complex, all with their merits. One attempted to explain it as the result of the transition period between 'natural' (or biological) living and 'artificial' (or machine) living. It concluded that until the 'artificial' became the natural and human psychology altered accordingly we should experience many such disturbances.

It was a likely explanation. But there might have been another, far simpler explanation.

Perhaps the world had just been—*bored*.

THE END